Circus Animals

Frank Gaimari

To my mother and father, whose love and guidance have shaped my world.

Contents

CIRCUS ANIMALS

1

MOLLY

AFTER ENDURING DAYS of solitude as a stowaway on the steamboat Natchez, the loud, shrill whistle heralded the end of my long journey. Emerging cautiously from my concealed spot behind weathered crates, I maneuvered my way through the legs of crew members and astonished passengers. As the gangway lowered, I seized the moment and dashed down the ramp.

A wave of exhilaration surged through me as my paws touched solid ground. I gazed up at the Saint Louis Cathedral, its tall spires reaching toward the sky, while the gardens of Jackson Square spread out before me. The enticing scents wafting from the nearby Market made my nose twitch and my stomach growl. After days without a meal, I knew exactly where to satisfy my hunger—the French Quarter.

Arriving on Bourbon Street was like jumping into a wild mix of sounds, lights, and excitement. The cobblestone streets buzzed with revelers, their laughter and chatter mixing with Zydeco music. Street performers entertained onlookers with impromptu acts while neon lights bathed everyone in a colorful glow. I felt alive, my tail wagging excitedly, eager to experience everything.

As I continued, the clatter of hooves caught my attention. I quickly stepped back as a horse-drawn carriage appeared, filled with humans immersed in laughter. As the carriage passed, a gasp caught in my throat.

From the crowd, a dogcatcher shrouded in darkness caught my attention. His long, greasy hair glistened under the streetlamps. Upon spotting me, he sneered and reached for his catchpole.

My instincts kicked into high gear as a sense of danger surged. With my heart pounding, I chose flight over confrontation and sprinted down the street.

The footsteps behind me sent a jolt of adrenaline coursing through my body. I maneuvered through the crowd, desperate to create distance between us. Yet the dogcatcher was relentless, his grasp on the pole unyielding. His heavy, labored breaths felt like a scorching flame on my tail as he drew ever closer, poised to strike at any moment. Panic washed over me in waves, engulfing me as I frantically scanned my surroundings, desperately searching for an escape from this terrifying chase.

Just then, I saw a glimmer of hope—a group of people catching Mardi Gras beads from an embellished balcony. I knew I had to make a run for it. Summoning every ounce of energy, I rushed toward them.

The dogcatcher lunged at me with a triumphant roar, but it was too late. I had made my escape by disappearing into the crowd. I saw him standing there, defeated, with his catchpole dangling lifelessly by his side.

Inhaling deeply, I dashed through the sea of legs toward a dimly lit alleyway, seeking sanctuary behind a dumpster. After a quick survey of my surroundings, relief washed over me as the dogcatcher was no longer in sight.

Sitting down, I calmed my racing heart. Yet, my peace was short-lived as a door swung open, flooding the alleyway with a bright light. Peeking cautiously from behind the dumpster, I noticed a man emerging from a restaurant. Clad in a work uniform and carrying a trash bag, his imposing figure caused me to cower, realizing he was approaching my location. Stuck in place, unable to flee, I was frozen when he confronted me.

"Don't be frightened. I won't hurt you," he muttered. "Are you hungry?" he continued.

Realizing he wasn't dangerous, I responded with a joyful, anticipatory bark as his question hung in the air.

The man's face lit up with a warm smile. Shortly after, he opened the large trash bag, which was bursting at its seams.

I watched as he began rummaging through it, his hand disappearing into its depths. After a few moments, he lifted a half-eaten sandwich.

"Look! A Muff! A muffuletta!"

His voice echoed off the alley walls as he held up the sandwich like a prize. The strange word rolled off his tongue and hung in the air, causing me to tilt my head in perplexity.

"You've never tasted one before?"

He expressed surprise in his tone, as if he couldn't comprehend my ignorance. In response, I shook my head, my ears flapping slightly with the motion. His surprise quickly morphed into enthusiasm as he saw an opportunity to share something he cherished.

"Well, it's only the best-tasting sandwich in New Orleans!" he proudly declared.

Just then, a jazz band marched past the alleyway, playing an upbeat tune. Completely caught up in the groove, the man beside me launched into an impromptu performance, singing about the sandwich.

"Grab a round loaf of bread. Add ham, salami, and cheese. Top it off with olive salad, and you'll have... a muffuletta."

I found myself drawn into the rhythm of the music and his enchanting description of the sandwich I had yet to savor. The word "muffuletta" danced on his lips as if invoking a spell of culinary delight, and before I knew it, we were moving together, caught in the joyous embrace of song and dance. My barks joined his singing, adding a playful note to the melody. It was a moment of pure silliness, yet it lifted my spirits, casting away the shadows in my heart.

"Come on... y'all. Raise your glass of sweet tea and toast the muffuletta. From Natchitoches to Lafayette and all the way down the line, the muffuletta reigns supreme. Muff... u... letta."

As the music dwindled and our little performance ended, the man, with a twinkle of anticipation in his eyes, offered me the remarkable gift—the muffuletta.

I eyed the sandwich with curiosity and hunger, unsure what to expect from this unfamiliar yet highly praised creation. My hesitation was brief, for the allure of the muffuletta was too compelling to resist.

With the first bite, my world transformed. The crusty exterior of the bread crunched satisfyingly under my teeth, giving way to a pillow-soft interior that welcomed the rich medley of flavors it encased. The cured meats were a revelation, their salty richness perfectly infused into every bite.

Then came the olive salad, a masterstroke of flavor that elevated the muffuletta from a mere sandwich to a work of art. Its tangy, vinegary zest cut through the richness of the meats, introducing a refreshing burst of brightness that made each bite an adventure.

As I savored the muffuletta, the man's interest in my identification tag sparked an unexpected connection. The small, metallic disc became the bridge between two worlds. As he leaned in, the light caught the surface of the tag, making it gleam amidst the shadows.

"Molly," he mumbled.

Hearing my name spoken filled me with indescribable joy. It was as if, in saying my name, he had acknowledged my existence. My response was instinctual, a bark that was more than just a sound—an outpouring of happiness.

"Well, enjoy your meal, little one. I have work to do," he muttered.

His voice carried a tenderness that made my heart swell.

As he waved goodbye, I barked again, my canine way of expressing thanks and appreciation for his kindness.

Then the man turned around, his muscles straining as he heaved the hefty trash bag into the dumpster. He waved again and moved toward the restaurant. As the door closed behind him, leaving me alone, I couldn't help but feel a newfound sense of warmth and connection.

Once a mere passageway filled with shadows and discarded things, the alleyway had transformed into a place of comfort.

◆◆◆

A sudden snarl sliced through the quiet alleyway as I savored my sandwich, causing me to freeze mid-chew. My ears perked up, fear washed over me, and my body stiffened. With trepidation, I raised my gaze, only to encounter a view that sent chills coursing through me.

Standing at the alleyway's entrance was an intimidating Rottweiler, his massive head held high and his muscular frame casting a formidable shadow. He pulled back his lips in a snarl, revealing a set of gleaming white teeth that contrasted starkly against his dark fur.

"I'll finish that sandwich for you."

With a deep and menacing voice, he resonated with an undercurrent of threat, making my fur stand on end. His gaze locked onto the remnants of the muffuletta, and I saw a dangerous mix of hunger and aggression reflected in his eyes.

With teeth that resembled weapons more than anything else, saliva dripped menacingly from his scowling expression. The sight made me yelp in fear, and I instinctively backed away and left the sandwich behind.

As despair consumed me, a yellow Labrador appeared out of nowhere. He blocked my path, positioning himself between me and the intimidating intruder. His protective stance acted as a shield, guarding me.

The Labrador was a striking figure. His athletic build and taller stature made him a formidable opponent of the intimidating Rottweiler. His coat, a radiant shade of golden yellow, gleamed under the dim light. He stood firm. His strength and determination were clear in his posture, signaling that he was not to be underestimated.

The ensuing clash between the two male dogs was intense. Their barks and snarls echoed through the alleyway, each sound punctuating the gravity of their struggle. The Rottweiler, imposing in stature, displayed valor in the fight. His strong jaws snapped fiercely, and his muscular frame surged forward to establish superiority. However, he quickly found himself overpowered by the Labrador, who swiftly pinned him down.

"Give up?" the Lab demanded, his voice echoing with a tone of finality that resonated through the tense air.

The defeated Rottweiler nodded in submission, acknowledging the Labrador's victory in this battle for supremacy.

"Now, find your dinner elsewhere," the Labrador commanded, releasing his grip on the vanquished dog. His tone was firm but devoid of cruelty, asserting his authority without unnecessary aggression.

I watched the entire spectacle in awe, my eyes wide with amazement. A yellow Labrador had defeated a Rottweiler, considered one of the most formidable breeds. The Labrador's tail wagged excitedly as the Rottweiler retreated from the alleyway, a clear testament to his victorious spirit.

He introduced himself.

"I'm Axle!"

Though imbued with strength, his voice carried an undercurrent of warmth and friendliness, starkly contrasting the tense atmosphere that had just moments ago filled the alleyway.

Grateful for his timely intervention, I smiled and gently kissed his snout. It seemed we connected instantly, as though he could sense my loneliness. With him by my side, the fear of being alone dissipated. Filled with appreciation, I shared my sandwich with him as a gesture of thanks, sealing our newfound friendship.

2

———————

AXLE

V ISITING THE CITY and hearing so much about the French Quarter, I felt compelled to explore it. Bourbon Street was teeming with people from all walks of life, creating a mosaic of colors and a medley of intriguing smells. The street's festivities had a mysterious allure that drew everyone in. Molly and I found ourselves swept along by the lively crowd.

Laughter and chatter filled the air, occasionally interrupted by applause as objects fell from balconies overhead. I watched humans reach up, their faces glowing with anticipation, eager to catch these items. Molly explained the crowd was catching plastic beads, and upon focused observation, I realized that the aim was to gather as many around your neck as possible. Intrigued by the concept, we joined in the excitement. We grabbed two strings of beads, wearing them with pride, feeling like we were part of the celebration.

I had experienced nothing quite like this before. While it was undoubtedly entertaining, a part of me was eager to move on. Our ultimate destination amidst this bustling carnival of sights and sounds was Café du Monde, the world-renowned coffee shop famed for its delectable coffee and beignets.

As Molly and I distanced ourselves from Bourbon Street's vibrant chaos, the music's pulsating rhythm gradually faded into a distant hum. The sudden tranquility allowed us to converse without raising our voices over the cacophony of sounds.

"I'm with the traveling circus," I mentioned.

"Are you a performer?" she asked.

I shook my head and chuckled lightly. "No, I'm just a watchdog, or better yet... a glorified babysitter." To my surprise, Molly responded with pride and excitement.

"I'm an acrobat!" she declared. "I can do flips, somersaults, and hop on my hind legs."

She recounted her past as a magician's sidekick, performing at parties and social events. However, a sadness washed over her as she mentioned her previous owner. Sensing her grief, I gently prodded about her human companion.

"The big storm separated us," she confessed, her voice barely above a whisper.

The way she referred to the storm showed it was a significant event that had profoundly disrupted her life. "You mean you haven't found your way home yet?" I asked, trying to understand her predicament.

"Well, yes..." her voice trailed off.

She left me intrigued yet puzzled. I sensed more of her story but didn't want to push her. I gave her space and waited for her to continue.

"The storm destroyed my home," she revealed, her words heavy with pain. "They tore it down. My owner is no longer there."

My heart ached with compassion as I listened to her recount her tale of loss and displacement.

She continued, telling me about her time in an animal shelter, her relocation to a different city, and her subsequent adoption by an elderly woman. However, her new home's impermanence soon became apparent when her owner's health deteriorated, and they sent her to a care facility. Not wanting to be displaced again, Molly stowed away on the Natchez steamboat and returned to New Orleans.

Her resilience and determination made me feel compelled to offer her a home. "You know, the circus is always looking for new performers," I suggested, wanting to bring hope into her world.

"Really?" Molly perked up, her eyes sparkling with newfound excitement at the prospect.

"YOU'RE NOT GETTING AWAY THIS TIME!"

We spun around in shock, our eyes landing on the menacing figure—the dogcatcher.

The man was brandishing his catchpole, his presence an unexpected and unwelcome threat. We instinctively recoiled from him. Reacting quickly, we dodged the firm grasp of his catchpole, leaping away just in time to escape its unforgiving grip.

"Run!" Molly shouted.

Without hesitation, we bolted, darting down the street with the fear of capture spurring us on. The swishing sound of the catchpole slicing through the air behind us was a terrifying reminder of our pursuer. It grew louder and more menacing with each passing second, urging us to run faster.

"He's catching up!" I yelled, noticing Molly was lagging. My heart hammered in my chest as I made a quick decision. Bending down,

I grabbed her by the scruff of her neck. She yelped in surprise but quickly understood my intention. With Molly safely out of harm's reach and a renewed sense of urgency fueling me, I mustered all my strength and sprinted faster.

I quickly turned a corner, darting into a narrow side alley to evade the dogcatcher. Discovering a flight of stairs leading to a hidden area, I gently set Molly down.

Holding our breath, we watched from our hideaway, praying the dogcatcher wouldn't find us. Our hearts pounded with relief as he sprinted past, oblivious to our location. We allowed ourselves to breathe only when he was well out of sight, our hearts racing from the high-stakes chase.

After we regained our composure, I suggested we continue our journey to the coffee shop. Both of us were now more aware than ever of the challenges ahead.

Exiting the alley, we raced down the street, scanning for any signs of danger. A feeling of relief washed over us when we spotted the sign for Café du Monde. We had found refuge from the dogcatcher's grasp.

Standing on the bustling sidewalk outside Café du Monde, I caught the attention of a busy server with a bark. He looked at us, his expression softening as he understood our plea for food. With a nod, he guided us to the back of the restaurant, away from the crowd of customers.

To our surprise, he flipped a cardboard box upside down, transforming it into a makeshift table.

"I'll be right back with something special," he promised, disappearing into the café.

After an eternity, he returned, holding a bowl of rich, dark chicory coffee and a plate bearing four golden-brown beignets generously dusted with powdered sugar. The sight of the treats made our mouths water in anticipation, our noses twitching at the delicious aroma wafting from the plate.

"Enjoy!"

I barked in reply, expressing my gratitude in the only way I knew how. To my surprise, his face lit up with understanding.

"You're welcome," he responded warmly and entered the restaurant.

The kindness of this human filled our hearts with immense joy. Looking at the beignets, I confessed, "I've never tasted one before."

"They're delicious," Molly assured me.

Curiosity getting the better of me, I leaned in to inspect the pastry covered in a snowy blanket of powdered sugar. Drawing in a deep breath, I inadvertently inhaled some of the powder, which caused me to sneeze violently.

A cloud of white erupted from the deep-fried pastry and flew into the air.

Seeing me covered in sugar was too much for Molly, and she burst into laughter. Her merriment was contagious, and soon I joined in. Our shared amusement echoed through the alleyway. This unexpected hilarity formed an instant bond between us, a memory that would forever cement our friendship.

◆◆◆

Fueled by the invigorating chicory coffee, our spirits rose as we continued our journey to the circus grounds. Navigating the streets of New Orleans, we stumbled upon a restaurant alive with the pulsating rhythms of live music. We paused, deciding to indulge in one last fun moment before reaching our destination.

The band played an upbeat American rhythm and blues song, its lyrics a vivid homage to the city's vibrant culture and spirit.

The infectious beat instantly captivated Molly. She began singing along, her voice blending harmoniously with the melody. Then, to my amazement, she stood up on her hind legs and started dancing. Her movements mirrored her excitement for life as she animatedly and energetically danced.

Catching my eye, she gestured for me to join her. Inspired by her uninhibited joy, I couldn't resist. I stood up and, letting go of all reservations, joined her. Together, we sang and danced with complete abandon, our movements complementing each other's.

Our laughter rang out, merging with the music as we swayed together. Passersby stopped to watch, their faces lighting up with smiles at our performance. Some even clapped along, adding to the festive atmosphere. Eventually, exhausted from our energetic display, we collapsed onto the pavement, panting and laughing. Despite our fatigue, a bubble of joy and satisfaction enveloped us.

The musicians gave us an appreciative nod, their tunes having found unexpected dancers.

Lying there, catching our breath under the night sky, we felt deeply connected to each other and the vibrant city around us. Our adventure had taken on a magical quality, turning an ordinary evening into an unforgettable memory we'd cherish forever.

◆◆◆

As we approached the circus grounds, the early morning sun painted the sky in hues of gold and orange. The enchanting melody of carnival music filled the air, beckoning us closer with its lively tune. Molly's eyes sparkled with excitement as she beheld the fascinating sights.

In the distance, a tightrope walker dressed in a dazzling uniform precariously balanced on a wire suspended high above the ground. His movements were fluid and confident, each step a testament to his incredible skill and courage. Nearby, a contortionist executed a series of impressive backflips, her agile body bending and twisting with an ease that left us awestruck. The spectacle of talent and daring feats had Molly staring in wide-eyed wonder, her anticipation building for what other surprises this magical place held.

As we ventured deeper into the bustling midway, a bright red ball suddenly rolled toward us. Before we could react, a figure darted out and scooped it up. We watched in awe as the man, a juggler, launched the ball into the air along with several others. His movements were swift and athletic, his hands a blur as he effortlessly kept the balls aloft.

However, the unyielding force of gravity inevitably intervened. The balls began their downward journey one by one, plummeting toward the ground with disappointing thuds.

"Darn it!" the juggler exclaimed in frustration.

His voice echoed through the bustling midway, a testament to his faltered performance. His brows furrowed in annoyance, reflecting his disappointment.

"As you can see, we all have roles here. I'm in charge of the nursery," I explained, hoping to give her a sense of the structure that held the circus together.

A confrontation between two circus members abruptly diverted our attention.

Sam, a seasoned circus carney, engaged in a heated exchange with Philip Andrews, the flamboyant ringmaster. Never one to shy away from theatrics, Philip donned his signature bright suit, a riot of colors and sequins that shimmered under the sunlight. He completed his ensemble with a grand top hat and a satin cravat, starkly contrasting Sam's casual, worn-out jeans and grungy T-shirt.

Amidst the festive atmosphere of the bustling midway, they stood, embodying a picture of strained nerves. With determination carved into his face, Philip extended an envelope toward Sam. The carney's hands trembled as he unfolded the paper.

His eyes narrowed as he read the bold words, forming a frown and knitting his eyebrows together in a scowl of displeasure. His fingers clenched around the letter, crumpling it as he fought to contain his rising anger. The letter's contents were clearly unwelcome, jolting the veteran carney out of his usual composure.

"How dare you!" Sam's voice thundered, thrusting the letter aggressively toward Philip. "You can't lower my pay. I've dedicated ten years to this circus!"

Philip's response cut through the tension like a knife, his voice laced with a biting condescension. "Oh, spare me your indignation," he snarled, barely flinching at Sam's outburst. "Boo-hoo," Philip mocked, his tone dripping with derision. "You're the world's worst circus barker. I have tolerated your mediocrity for far too long."

The ringmaster's words were venomous, delivering a blow that visibly shook Sam.

"And another thing," he continued, his icy gaze piercing. "Your long service means nothing if your performance doesn't match up. It's high time you faced the music."

Sam's face contorted in outrage. Pointing a finger, "You'll regret this," he vowed, his stance firm and gaze unyielding.

Tension filled the air as the conflict reached a boiling point, leaving bystanders anxious about the unfolding drama.

Turning to Molly, I explained that the circus was grappling with financial woes, my expression darkening at the thought of how much had changed. "Because of our difficulties," I shared, "the ringmaster has converted the nursery into a petting zoo."

"That's dreadful!" she gasped.

"I know," I lamented. "It's a dire situation. But believe it or not, the babies will do their part."

As our walk continued, Molly noticed a sign that read, "Endangered Amur Leopard." We stopped to look inside a cage on a flatbed truck. "This is Taya," I whispered.

The panting leopard lying on her side glanced down at us.

"Why is she breathing so hard?" Molly asked concerned.

As I prepared to explain, Molly turned and noticed a golden retriever crawling from underneath the truck. She gasped at his beautiful mahogany coat, distinctive lion's mane, and muscular frame.

"She's breathing hard because she's in labor," the dog exclaimed.

Molly gasped in awe as I explained the rarity of the Amur Leopard species. With only eighty-four leopards left in the world, her baby was a miracle.

I introduced Molly to Chief, mentioning that his job was to protect Taya and her unborn cub. After the introduction, Chief started giggling and playfully pounced on me. We had known each other since we were puppies, and we filled our bond with an everlasting love for one another. As Chief pinned me down, I told Molly, between bursts of laughter, that he would be a father soon.

"Are you having a boy or girl?" Molly asked.

"A boy," Chief revealed with pride. "We've already named him Capo."

"Does that mean anything?"

Chief stopped roughhousing, smiled, and replied, "It's Italian for 'Chief.' I've given him my name!"

Molly gasped in delight.

While Chief and I reveled in our play, Molly found an unusual sight that drew her attention. Morton, a mouse of considerable girth, emerged from the straw-covered cage floor. He yawned, stretching his paws upward. His fur, a mottled mix of gray and white, was unkempt and disheveled because of its uneven distribution.

Morton stood and pushed his way through the narrow bars of the cage, his ample belly barely squeezing through. Once free, he paused, his beady eyes glaring with an intensity that was hard to ignore.

"Can't you see I'm trying to sleep here?"

Seconds later, he leaped from the cage, landing with a thud on the ground.

"It's far too early for such nonsense."

Morton approached us, only to find himself suddenly under Chief's colossal paw. His eyes widened in an exaggerated display of terror as he peered upwards. He gasped loudly, raising his front paws theatrically.

"Noooo…" Morton swooned.

Chief stopped playing as Morton collapsed, staring at him in disbelief. The tension hung in the air until Chief, unable to hold back any longer, broke the silence.

"Must you always be so dramatic?" He chided, rolling his eyes.

"Is he all right?" Molly asked, her voice laced with genuine concern as she looked at the still heap that was Morton.

"Oh, he's fine… just another Oscar-worthy performance," Chief replied, a chuckle rumbling deep in his throat.

I stifled a laugh as I witnessed the unfolding scene. Morton stirred, grasped his forehead, and released a theatrical, bewildered sigh.

"Where am I? What happened?"

"You fainted!" I explained as Chief nipped my ear and led me around. I couldn't help but grin with delight at my best friend's mischief while Morton shook his head, continuing his dramatic display.

"These two never stop playing," Morton sighed, raising his paws dramatically before muttering that it was time for breakfast. "I'm outta here!" he shouted, running away on his hind legs.

With an amused gasp, Chief watched Morton's dramatic exit while I suppressed my giggles at the comical scene.

Molly smiled at the mouse's retreat. Then, her gaze shifted toward Taya, the pregnant leopard.

"I've always dreamed of having a family of my own," She confessed, her voice filled with longing.

Taya offered a nod of understanding. "Motherhood is indeed a beautiful journey," she responded, her smile tender and encouraging.

Our laughter disrupted their sincere conversation, returning their attention to our playful wrestling match. They joined in our laughter, their shared merriment echoing throughout the midway.

◆◆◆

I informed Molly that my workday would start soon because the babies were expected at the nursery. She gasped, visibly excited about meeting them. As we walked toward the pen, we reveled in the serene morning.

Upon reaching the entrance, I pointed to the sign above the gate that read "Petting Zoo." When I turned to Molly, her face was filled with shock.

"These little ones deserve more respect," she protested, her voice laden with contempt for their commercial exploitation.

I reassured Molly that I did everything possible to ensure their happiness, which helped ease some of her worries.

As we entered the enclosure, two lion cubs followed us, their eyes alight with youthful curiosity. The larger cub, noticing Molly's attention, sat back on his hind legs and raised his paws toward me.

"Put 'em up!" the cub roared playfully—his tiny voice filled with faux ferocity.

I joined in his game. Our boxing match was a delightful echo of my childhood memories. The cub—Jett—eagerly sparred with me, his tiny paws connecting with mine in a lively dance.

"You're feeling feisty this morning!" I ribbed him, only for him to respond with a playful uppercut to my chin.

"He's precious!" Molly exclaimed.

Jett, not wanting to be seen as just "precious," puffed out his chest in pride before wandering off. His brother, Harry, approached us. I lowered myself to the ground, allowing him to clamber onto my back.

Struggling to keep his balance, he finally stood tall and declared himself the "King of the Mountain" before tumbling to the ground in a soft heap.

I gently assessed his condition by tickling his belly, ensuring he was unharmed. "Good morning, Harry!"

"Hi, Axle!" Harry murmured with a giggle.

Upon confirming Harry's safety, the resonating sound of a loud trumpet captivated our focus. Elsa, the baby elephant, came barreling into the pen.

She was an adorable sight, her large ears flapping joyously and her small trunk swinging as she halted, gleefully stomping in a mud puddle. Despite her muddy antics, her infectious joy was irresistible.

A sudden shriek drew our attention to Mia, the baby giraffe, as she deftly avoided Elsa's enthusiastic frolics in the mud. She was enchanting with her long, slender legs and large, curious eyes.

Bounding into the pen, a baby zebra interrupted our laughter with his high spirits. He kicked his hooves playfully and eagerly announced his excitement to pl-pl-play with his new friends. I introduced him to Molly as Luca, our latest addition from the New Orleans Zoo.

Just as we were soaking in the heartwarming scene, disaster struck. In his eagerness to play, Luca ran over to Jett without noticing Harry in his path and accidentally bumped into him. Harry tumbled to the ground, wailing in distress.

"It-it… was an accident," Luca said apologetically.

He looked so sorry that it melted our hearts. Mia looked at him perplexedly, confused about why he constantly repeated his words. Elsa then stepped in and explained that it was a speech disorder called stuttering.

I nodded in agreement, adding that they should listen to him patiently. Mia murmured understanding before turning to Elsa, who had a plan brewing in her head.

"Let's look for a four-leaf clover!"

Excited by their newfound mission, they scampered into the pen, momentarily forgetting about Harry's cries. I bent down to Harry's level, my voice soft, and asked if he was okay. After briefly hesitating, he nodded, managing a tiny, squeaky "yes." However, his brave facade crumbled when his brother told him to "toughen up," inadvertently causing another round of tears.

Jett groaned exasperatedly, unsure of how to console his brother.

Feeling sympathy for Luca, who lingered apologetically on the sidelines, I shifted my focus. "Everyone, gather around! Elsa, Mia, I need you here as well!" I called—my voice authoritative.

Elsa and Mia exchanged reluctant glances.

"You can search for a four-leaf clover afterward. I want you to meet someone."

Realizing my intentions, they smiled and joined the group clustering around us.

I introduced Molly and shared her story of aspiration and dreams—how she longed to join the circus as an acrobat.

Molly's tale captivated the babies, causing them to pause their antics and listen with rapt attention. Their eyes sparkled with curiosity and wonder, their initial squabbles temporarily forgotten as they envisioned Molly performing daring feats high above the ground, somersaulting through the air with effortless grace.

Intrigued by the prospect of acrobatics, Mia inquired about Molly's act.

Thrilled to share her talent, Molly stepped back with a wag of her tail, creating enough space for her performance. Then, defying all expectations, she launched herself into a handstand. Her muscular front legs held her weight effortlessly, her body forming a perfect line against the sky. Watching her perform a handstand was a delightful surprise, causing the babies to gasp in astonishment.

Molly had not yet finished. She flipped back onto her paws and precisely executed a series of backflips, arcing her body beautifully through the air before landing perfectly on the ground. The spectacle left the young audience wide-eyed and open-mouthed with wonder.

Molly stopped, panting lightly, her chest heaving with exertion. Yet, the twinkle in her eye and wide grin made it clear—she loved every moment.

The babies watched, enthralled, their eyes brimming with pure delight. Inspired by Molly's performance, Jett attempted to replicate her backflip. Though awkward at best, his attempt ended with him landing on his furry bottom. Yet, his spirit remained undeterred as he enthusiastically got up for another try.

Harry, the cautious one, watched his brother's failed attempt with wide-eyed wonder. After a moment of hesitation, he gave it a shot himself. He launched into the air with a roar that sounded like a squeak. However, instead of performing a front flip, he managed a clumsy somersault, ending on his back, his tiny paws flailing in the air. His antics brought about a round of giggles from everyone.

Elsa, the elephant, observed the scene keenly, pondering if she could replicate such an act. She tried to roll over, but her hefty frame made the task challenging. Instead, she ended up playfully splattering more mud around.

Mia, the giraffe calf, was too tall to attempt a backflip and didn't want to be left out of the fun. She bent her long legs and tried to do a cartwheel. While her attempt was far from successful, it added to the overall merriment, eliciting chuckles from her audience.

Luca, forgetting his earlier mishap, bounced around excitedly. He attempted a sequence of progressively higher jumps. His hooves were ill-suited for such acrobatics, leading him to tumble onto the cushioned grass surface. However, undeterred by the setback, he promptly got up, ready to make another attempt, his enthusiasm undimmed.

Observing these youngsters' exuberant laughter and joyful attempts filled me with profound satisfaction. The babies received genuine love and proper attention despite the petting zoo's commercial motives.

When Molly finally came over, panting but radiating satisfaction, I praised her, "That was great!" She responded with a happy wag of her tail. As we returned to the babies, I couldn't help but smile broadly. These moments made my job worthwhile, a beautiful reminder of the joy and innocence that filled our daily lives.

3

MOLLY

AS ELSA, MIA, and I meandered through the pen in search of a four-leaf clover, we suddenly found ourselves under the intense scrutiny of three dogs—a Jack Russell, a Scottish Terrier, and a poodle of considerable size. The Poodle's towering stature made my petite figure seem even smaller. Their intense gazes were disconcerting, creating an unexpected sense of self-consciousness within me.

The Jack Russell was quite a handsome fellow. His white fur, accentuated with tan patches, added a rugged charm to his overall appearance. He was the first to break the silence, his voice smooth as he complimented someone on their beauty. It took a few moments to realize that he was complimenting me.

The Scottish Terrier, a sturdy little dog with short legs and a dense black coat, seemed as surprised as I was by the Jack Russell's comment.

"Marceau?" The Terrier exclaimed.

A rush of warmth spread through me at Marceau's compliment. However, the large poodle abruptly interrupted my moment of joy. His fur, perfectly styled in a distinctive French trim, was a striking shade of gray. His accent carried a distinct French lilt. Looking down his nose at me, he made a snide remark about my appearance, suggesting a flea dip might be in order. The comment was so ludicrous that it was hard not to chuckle despite the blush creeping up my cheeks.

Amused by the spectacle, the Scottish Terrier pointed out that Marceau had never acted like this. "I think he's in love!" he declared, chuckling.

The Poodle, clearly feeling slighted, scoffed with jealousy. "We're the same breed! She should be interested in me!"

Ignoring the Poodle's grand proclamation, I locked eyes with Marceau. I could feel my face reddening further under his gaze.

Marceau returned my stare with a tender smile as if he understood what was going through my mind. Meanwhile, the Poodle, ever the comic relief, was busy fussing over his top knot and muttering about his looks.

"Do you think she finds me attractive?" he implored the Scottish Terrier.

The Terrier's response was blunt and to the point. "Dude, she's not into you!"

The Poodle gradually realized it as he saw my gaze on Marceau. Just then, a triumphant shriek echoed through the pen. We all turned to see Elsa holding a four-leaf clover, her trunk waving it around like a victory flag.

"I found one!" Elsa exclaimed proudly.

Mia stepped forward and smelled it.

"It doesn't smell." Elsa clarified.

I explained to them that finding a four-leaf clover was good luck and that everyone should make a wish. Luca overheard our conversation and joined us.

"Will the wish come true?" he asked, his eyes wide with curiosity.

I smiled warmly. "If you wish hard enough," I reassured him.

As Mia took the clover from Elsa, her eyes squeezed shut in deep concentration. The silence was intense as everyone waited for her wish. When she finally opened her eyes, they sparkled with excitement, and she let out an infectious, giddy laugh.

"I wished for a baby brother!" she exclaimed.

Her innocent wish sparked laughter, a light-hearted happiness that warmed our hearts.

Then, it was Luca's turn. He accepted the clover with quiet reverence, settling down on his haunches. His boyish face became serious as he closed his eyes, focusing all his energy on his wish. When he finally opened them, they were soft with a kind of heartrending contentment.

Everyone watched in silent anticipation, waiting for him to reveal his desire.

"I wished to see my mother again."

His words hung heavy in the air, their weight silencing the laughter that had filled the pen moments ago. My heart ached to hear such a profound longing from this boy. His wish, so simple yet painfully out of reach, was a stark reminder of these babies' harsh realities.

Out of the corner of my eye, I saw Philip Andrews, the circus ringmaster, distributing sealed envelopes to the performers standing nearby. As each performer read the contents, their expressions changed from curiosity to shock. The dread that swept over their faces was clear, adding another layer of sorrow to the already somber atmosphere.

Marceau's confident demeanor and resonant voice immediately caught my attention as he entered the pen, and I found myself irresistibly drawn to his captivating presence.

"Could I interest you in a tour of the circus grounds this evening?"

Marceau's words sent a wave of exhilaration washing over me. Each syllable caressed my senses, igniting a tingly sensation that was impossible to ignore. A playful smile appeared on my face, and I nodded eagerly.

"I'll see you tonight," he grinned.

Just as Marceau exited the pen and rejoined his companions, Elsa approached, clutching the four-leaf clover. She chuckled softly—her eyes alight with mischief as she passed me the lucky charm. She seemed to know what my wish would be.

I accepted the clover.

My lips curved into a smile as I closed my eyes. Holding it close, I envisioned a future where Marceau was steadfastly by my side. A vivid image unfolded in my mind—a cozy doghouse adorned with a white picket fence and puppies frolicking in the yard.

This thought of a beautiful future with Marceau warmed my heart, filling it with an overwhelming sense of warmth and happiness. Clasping the clover tightly in my paw, I hoped that this wish, this dream of a life brimming with love and laughter alongside Marceau, would one day become my reality.

4

BOBBI-CAT

A
S DUSK BATHED the sky in shades of purple and orange. It signaled the commencement of a cherished routine between Morton and me. Each evening, we'd indulge in an exhilarating game of cat-and-mouse, where I assumed the role of the pursuer, and Morton became my perpetually elusive prey. He reveled in the thrill and drama of our game, his laughter echoing through the air as he evaded my attempts to catch him.

Upon reaching Taya's cage, I noticed two familiar figures—Philip Andrews, the domineering ringmaster, and Sofia Bartolini, the captivating ring mistress. Taya's discomfort was obvious as her eyes flickered nervously from one corner of the cage to another, her instincts sensing something amiss in the ringmaster's presence.

Morton made his presence known by suddenly popping his head from the cage floor, only to withdraw quickly at the sight of the ringmaster. His actions were a testament to the fear that Philip instilled in everyone.

Seeking refuge under a nearby truck, I found myself hidden from view. My fur, an intricate pattern of black, gray, and brown stripes, offered perfect camouflage against the encroaching darkness. I strained my ears to catch the conversation between the humans.

"I want a large banner that reads, 'The Only Baby Amur Leopard on Earth,'" the ringmaster demanded, his voice echoing enthusiastically. "This baby leopard will bring us financial success—a gold mine!" he exclaimed. "I want this banner up as soon as the cub is born," he ordered.

Sofia's response was a disappointed nod, her silence speaking volumes about her disagreement with his audacious plans.

As Philip exited, my gaze followed him, a chill running down my spine. I knew all too well that he had malevolent intentions and only tolerated my presence for rodent control. He threatened starvation if I failed to fulfill my "duties," an act of cruelty that was fortunately mitigated by Sofia's kind heart. She empathized with my reluctance to kill, understanding that it wasn't in my nature, and fed me every night.

Stepping out from under the truck, my eyes couldn't help but linger on Sofia. Nothing could capture the mesmerizing beauty she possessed. Her Italian heritage was clear in her flawless, sun-kissed skin that radiated warmth. Cascading down her back in shiny waves, her long, ebony hair framed her face and enhanced her enchanting appeal. Her features were sharp and striking—high cheekbones, a perfectly sculpted nose, almond-shaped eyes that held a world of emotions, full lips, and a jawline that exuded strength. Sofia was a beacon of beauty, a vision that could captivate anyone fortunate to cross her path.

"Hi, Bobbi-Cat!" She greeted me warmly.

I meowed in return.

She picked me up, turned me over, and kissed my belly. Right away, I purred.

"I don't know how the ringmaster thought you were a boy," Sofia murmured, shaking her head.

Once again, I meowed to express that he was a foolish man.

When I arrived at the circus, the ringmaster named me Bobcat. He thought I was a boy because my tail was shorter than most. I had lost part of it in a fight. I meowed, telling him he was wrong, but he couldn't understand me. When he introduced me to Sofia, she immediately realized the mistake and renamed me Bobbi-Cat.

While comfortably nestled in Sofia's protective embrace, a burst of raucous laughter caught my attention. My gaze shifted toward the noise source, landing on the circus carneys, Sam and his companion, Billy-Joe.

Their behavior seemed suspiciously out of place, and their laughter rang too loud in the tranquil evening. Intrigued, I wondered what caused their unusual mirth.

Billy-Joe was an intriguing character. His naivety often eclipsed his amiable nature, rendering him susceptible to manipulation.

His physical appearance did him no favors, either. With his stained, missing, and crooked teeth, his poor oral hygiene was obvious, making everyone cringe when he smiled.

While the circus carnies raised my eyebrows, a bustling scene abruptly diverted my attention. Looking up, I saw Frank and George, the two Black-Crowned Heron birds, engaged in their typically humorous banter. Sofia also shifted her gaze skyward, her eyes shimmering with curiosity despite not understanding the avian dialogue.

George was grumbling about his hungry stomach, his voice laced with irritation. Frank launched a detailed lecture on the dangers of eating food from the concession stand, particularly its tendency to induce gas. Their ludicrous exchange was so amusing that I had to stifle a laugh.

"Everything makes you fart!" George snapped back.

Landing on the concession stand roof, George used his wing and pointed at a slice of pie that someone had discarded.

Frank squinted, struggling to focus on George's point. His bewilderment was clear. "You know I'm nearsighted. What are you pointing at?"

"The pie! In the trash can?" George said, his voice dripping with impatience.

Once Frank finally noticed the cherry pie, he exclaimed, "Oh no!" with exaggerated drama. "The last time I ate a cherry, I suffered terribly! My stomach cramped, and I had diarrhea."

"Enough!" George cut him off, unable to endure another of Frank's drawn-out stories of gastric woes.

Taken aback by George's bluntness, Frank's eyes bulged. "Geez... I was just suggesting I might be allergic."

George fixed his gaze on the pie, his anticipation clear. Suddenly, his tongue darted out, grazing his beak with a hint of impatience. Then he looked at Frank, who was theatrically massaging his knee, loudly bemoaning his battle with arthritis in a tone rich with melodrama. Unable to contain his irritation, George fluttered his wings in an exasperated display.

"You're such a hypochondriac!"

Stung by George's candid remark, Frank muttered under his breath but nonetheless trailed after him to the trash bin.

Suddenly, Taya's agonized cry pierced the tranquil evening, signaling that the birth of her cub was imminent. Turning to Taya's cage, I caught sight of Morton, who sprang up like a jack-in-the-box from the straw-covered floor.

"Oh, my goodness!" he shrieked, his voice a high-pitched squeal as he bounced around in sheer panic, completely at a loss for what to do.

Seeing him reduced to a bundle of nerves was both hilarious and heartwarming.

"I need you to relax!" Taya pleaded, her voice filled with pain and urgency. She then let out a roar, calling for Sofia's help.

The ring mistress, always calm and composed, quickly assessed the situation. She set me down and instructed Chief to find the ringmaster and inform him of the unfolding drama.

Chief hurried away, urgently announcing, "The baby's coming! The baby's coming!"

Meanwhile, George, the Black-Crowned Heron, was buzzing with excitement. Caught indecision, he wavered between flying over to Taya's cage or waiting for his friend Frank, who was utterly engrossed in his cherry.

"Quit dawdling!" George called out. "We're going to miss the birth!" He continued, soaring into the air.

Frank hastily finished his cherry and flew after him.

As Sofia opened the cage to attend the impending birth, anticipation spread through the crowd of gathered performers. They watched in hushed silence, their faces lit with fascination and apprehension.

However, amidst this sea of faces, Sam and Billy-Joe's sinister snickers pierced the atmosphere like a sharp knife. Their presence was ominous, and their laughter was a jarring contrast to the otherwise joyous ambiance.

As the two carneys huddled together, whispering fervently, I narrowed my eyes, straining to catch snippets of their conversation.

"We'll show him!" Sam murmured under his breath, a malicious glint in his eyes. "He'll regret cutting our pay," he continued, his voice barely above a whisper.

"What exactly are you planning to do?" Billy-Joe asked, his eyebrows knitting together in a show of genuine concern.

"It's what we're... going to do." Sam corrected, his face breaking into a sly, conspiratorial smile.

"Oh..." Billy-Joe responded with uncertainty. He swallowed hard, his adam's apple bobbing nervously. "The plan?" His voice squeaked an octave higher, a clear testament to his anxiety.

In response, Sam slapped Billy-Joe's stomach, effectively silencing him. The sound echoed through the stillness, causing Billy-Joe to bend over and wince.

"Why did you do that?" he exclaimed, tenderly rubbing his belly. "That hurt!"

With a swift motion, Sam shushed him, pressing a finger to his lips. His eyes darted nervously, scanning their surroundings to ensure their conversation hadn't attracted unwanted attention.

Meanwhile, Taya's moans grew louder and more intense, marking the climax of labor. As she pushed with all her might, the gathered crowd held its collective breath. Suddenly, amidst the pain and struggle, a tiny cub emerged. My jaw dropped as I watched the newborn leopard enter the world.

For a moment, time seemed to stand still. Everyone stood rooted to their spots, amazed by the new life. Then, a soft, kitten-like sound echoed from the cage, breaking the silence and drawing everyone's attention.

Morton sat in the cage's corner, tears of happiness streaming down his face. The sight of the newborn cub moved him so deeply that he couldn't contain his emotions.

With a gentleness that belied her strength, Sofia reached for the little one. She cradled the cub in her arms—her face radiating love and pride. She then raised the cub high for everyone to see, her joy infectious. After sharing the moment with the crowd, she carefully nestled the baby beside her mother.

Taya, weary but satisfied, beamed as she declared, "My baby... Mischa."

As I stepped from the cage, I knew this poignant memory would stay with me forever. Inspired by the wonder of life, I set out to find

Cody, the Maine Coon cat who had captured my attention. It was time to conquer my shyness and express my feelings to him.

5

AXLE

AS MOLLY AND I stepped into the big top tent, its grandeur overwhelmed our senses. The tent was colossal, capable of accommodating hundreds of spectators, yet it exuded a captivating, intimate, cozy atmosphere. The red and white stripes adorning the sides seemed to ripple in a mesmerizing dance, creating a backdrop of vibrant color.

Looking up, a breathtaking sight greeted us. The ceiling blazed with hundreds of dazzling lights, casting an enchanting glow across the entire space. Majestic poles towered above us, standing tall and proud, effortlessly supporting the tent's weight.

Philip Andrews stood imposingly in the center ring, crossing his arms over his chest and wearing a stern expression as he observed three elephants attempting to execute a trick. Among them, Mabel, the mother of Elsa, was notably a giant. Her size was truly awe-inspiring—she was a magnificent creature that commanded attention. Her wrinkled and rough skin bore testament to her age and wisdom. Her long, curved tusks, capped with balls for safety, hinted at their inherent strength. Yet, she appeared to struggle to keep her balance, much to the visible irritation of the ringmaster. His exasperation grew with each unsuccessful attempt.

The air was tense as the elephants labored to perfect the trick. We watched anxiously, our hearts pounding, as these magnificent creatures tried desperately to please the harsh ringmaster.

"What's wrong with her?" Philip demanded, his voice echoing ominously through the tent.

The trainer responded with a whip snap, causing Mable to shiver in fear.

"Mable!" he shouted impatiently.

He snapped the whip again, sending a chill down my spine.

In response to the intimidating command, Mable leaned forward and placed her head against the ground, raising her hind legs in a heartbreaking display.

"Good girl!" the trainer murmured.

His elation was short-lived as Philip barked loudly, "Do you call this a circus act? I wouldn't pay money for this crap! I've seen enough..." His words hung heavy in the air. "What's wrong with her?" he continued, demanding an answer.

"She just had a baby, sir."

Philip threw his hands up in frustration. "A baby? That was three months ago. Don't you realize I have a show to put on?"

"Yes, sir!" the trainer stammered out.

"You're fired!"

"Sir?" the trainer muttered.

"Vacate the premises and summon the alternate trainer," Philip commanded.

His tone was stark and unyielding, leaving no room for a counter-argument.

As the disheartened elephant trainer retreated from the tent, a knot of worry formed in my stomach about Molly's well-being, given the ringmaster's notorious disposition. "Make this good, or he'll call the animal shelter," I warned. The words escaped my mouth no sooner than I realized my grave mistake.

Molly gasped—her eyes wide with terror.

Regret washed over me like a tidal wave, and I hastened to mollify my error, reassuringly saying, "You've got this... don't panic."

The ringmaster swiveled around abruptly and caught sight of us. He crossed his arms over his chest again, his piercing gaze questioning our presence. I nodded in Molly's direction, seeking confirmation of her readiness.

She reciprocated with a nervous nod.

Gathering my courage, I picked up a red ball and advanced toward the intimidating figure of the ringmaster.

"What have we here?" he sneered gruffly, looking at Molly with blatant repulsion. He raised his hands in disgust. "She's filthy! When was she last bathed?"

I let the ball drop from my mouth and pushed it toward him.

Philip stood there, frozen in shock, trying to decipher my silent request.

"Do you want me to throw the ball?" he queried incredulously.

I barked in affirmation, gesturing fervently toward Molly.

He threw his hands up in exasperation, sighed heavily, and rolled his eyes. "I don't have time for such frivolities," he declared dismissively.

Undeterred, I barked again, my plea growing more desperate.

"Oh, all right," he conceded guiltily.

He picked up the ball with another heavy sigh and tossed it haphazardly.

Molly sprinted forward and caught the ball on her nose. Balancing expertly on her hind legs, she hopped forward three times. However, she unexpectedly lost her footing and tumbled to the ground, causing the ball to roll toward the ringmaster.

I held my breath in nervous anticipation.

"Are you kidding me?" he exclaimed in disbelief.

As the new assistant trainer appeared in the ring, Philip Andrews pointed at Molly and instructed him to call the animal shelter.

"Yes, sir!" the assistant snapped to attention, his voice trembling.

Molly gasped with dread and bolted toward the ringmaster. Her small, fragile body quivered uncontrollably with fear, tears streaming down her face as she whimpered for another try.

"Oh, my," I murmured, watching intently.

Philip Andrews' steely gaze bore into Molly's tear-filled eyes. For a brief, fragile moment, his hardened exterior cracked. With a deep, reluctant sigh, he issued a final, ominous warning. "I'll give you one more chance. Fail me again… and you're finished!"

The ultimatum hung in the air.

The ringmaster grabbed the ball and tossed it into the air.

I held my breath, watching Molly lunge forward with lightning-fast reflexes to catch the ball on her nose. Moments later, I exhaled, seeing her hop forward three times on her hind legs.

"Woo-hoo! Whoopie!"

Philip Andrews watched, bored at first, but then became fascinated as Molly lowered the ball to the ground and performed a dizzying array of tricks—backflips, front flips, and somersaults.

Impressed, the ringmaster clapped his hands in delight. He realized Molly had the talent and the spirit to become a star performer. Turning to the assistant, he ordered, "Take her to the bathing tent."

I rushed over to Molly to offer my congratulations. However, Chief and the dog-faced boy burst into the ring before I could reach her. Excitement flushed the boy's face.

"Sir, sir," the boy cried breathlessly, "Taya had her baby!"

The ringmaster stood still, deep in thought. Soon, a grin spread across his face. He knew the circus would be financially secure now that Taya's baby had been born. Rubbing his hands excitedly, he instructed the assistant to secure the elephants before leaving.

The elephants trumpeted their irritation, and the assistant nodded in agreement. As Philip left the big top, I couldn't help but shake my head in frustration. "I'll talk to you later," I shouted to Molly and chased after the ringmaster.

6

MOLLY

M Y EYES SPARKLED with anticipation as the tub filled with soapy, bubbly water. Eagerly, I plunged into the bath, letting the scented suds envelop me. A contented sigh escaped as the warm, bubble-filled water caressed my fur. The caring woman attending to me gently scrubbed away grime and knots with a luxurious shampoo.

My occasional gleeful barks punctuated the entire delightful experience. The groomer's warm and kind demeanor and comforting smile assured me of her benevolence. I knew I could trust her. After bathing, I leaped out of the tub and shook off the water. Although the woman got soaked, she smiled and didn't seem upset. Once dry, she chose a vibrant circus outfit that fit perfectly and added a spritz of doggy perfume for an extra touch.

When she held up a hand mirror, tears moved me. "Look at me—I'm beautiful."

Although she couldn't understand my bark, she seemed to sense my happiness and enveloped me in a tender hug. My tail responded with wild wags to her affectionate gesture. After snuggling into her warmth, I barked again in thanks and scampered off to join Marceau for what promised to be an exciting evening.

◆◆◆

When I emerged from the bathing tent, I immediately attracted everyone's attention. With my fresh haircut and stylish outfit, I felt beautiful and radiated pure joy.

As I strolled past a woman of considerable size sitting in front of her trailer, her warm, welcoming smile caught my attention. Her face was round and adorned with rosy cheeks, radiating friendliness. Her eyes sparkled with kindness and seemed to hold a lifetime of stories.

Luxurious, thick, brown hair flowed down her shoulders, framing her face and adding an elegant touch to her overall appearance. She wore a flowing floral dress that exuded an air of softness and comfort. Despite her noticeable size and the nameplate on her trailer that read "Fat Lady," it didn't encapsulate her entirety. I knew the term was inappropriate and offensive, stirring sympathy within me. It contributed to weight-based discrimination and body shaming, failing to acknowledge the woman's warmth, kindness, and grace.

"You look mighty fine!" she exclaimed.

I expressed my gratitude with a grateful bark and leisurely approached her. She seemed sad sitting there alone, so I sat beside her and extended my paw in greeting. Of course, she couldn't understand my barks, but she seemed to grasp that I was introducing myself and shook my paw.

"Nice to meet you too! My name's Rosie," she said, scratching my ears affectionately.

It felt wonderful.

As she finished, I looked up at her and saw her warm smile. She seemed to enjoy our interaction. Her gaze shifted, and her face lit up as she spotted Marceau approaching us. She waved excitedly. I turned to see him, and my tail wagged with joy. He, too, had bathed and gotten a haircut. He looked handsome, reinforcing my attraction to him.

"Is this your friend?" Rosie asked.

I barked affirmatively as Marceau stopped and leaned against me. Rosie grinned, sensing our mutual affection.

"You make a perfect pair!" she exclaimed, delightfully clutching her heart.

Marceau and I both barked our thanks.

She laughed, understanding our canine language.

Once again, I barked to show my intention to return for a visit. I knew I couldn't converse with her, but I believed my presence would ease her loneliness.

"I'd like that!" she responded, comprehending my bark. "Come see me anytime!"

I nodded in agreement, and Marceau led me away, chattering excitedly about his plans for the evening. I cast one last glance back at Rosie and wagged my tail. She returned my smile, evidently happy for me as well.

7

AXLE

I RUSHED BACK to Taya's cage, beating the ringmaster to the punch. As I drew closer, I saw Chief gazing affectionately at the newborn baby—he had returned ahead of me. His face lit up when he saw me approaching, a warm, welcoming smile spreading across his features.

Arriving, I could barely contain my excitement as I looked at Taya. "Congratulations!" I exclaimed, my voice echoing around the enclosure.

The serene beauty of the baby utterly captivated me. "She's truly stunning," I said, my voice filled with genuine admiration and awe.

The baby was a perfect bundle of fur, her tiny paws twitching slightly in her sleep.

Hearing my words, Taya shifted her gaze from her baby to mine. A faint glimmer of pride appeared in her eyes as she responded.

"Thank you."

Her voice was soft and filled with love. Although her response was simple, it conveyed all her emotions.

"The miracle of life is amazing," Chief mumbled, his voice barely above a whisper.

Turning my attention to my best friend, I listened as he began talking about his wife and their shared excitement about becoming parents. A single tear escaped his eye as he spoke, tracing a path down his cheek. His vulnerability touched something deep within me, mirroring my joy for his upcoming journey into fatherhood. In return, I offered him a supportive smile.

Sofia exited the cage and stood beside us.

All eyes turned as the ringmaster barreled toward the cage, ranting about the financial implications. Sofia's face crinkled into a frown upon hearing his words. Clearly, she disapproved of his fixation on profits rather than appreciating the moment's beauty.

Despite the ringmaster's inappropriate behavior, the joy and happiness that came with the baby's birth were unmistakable. Sofia, Chief, and I celebrated as a family, our hearts full of love for this new addition.

As the evening progressed, I bade goodnight to Sofia and Chief while ignoring the ringmaster. They knew Luca was waiting for me. Normally, I slept at Sofia's doorstep to protect her, but with Luca's arrival, I needed to be with him. His nightmares of being separated from his mother disrupted his sleep, but he was fine if I lay beside him.

"I'll see you in the morning," I told Chief as a wave of anxiety overwhelmed me. I couldn't understand its meaning or why I was feeling this way. It was almost like a premonition of some sort. The fear gripped me so tightly that I felt compelled to acknowledge my friend.

"Thank you."

"For what?" Chief mumbled, tilting his head in bewilderment.

"Your friendship."

Chief responded to my words with a warm smile, declaring that I was the best friend anyone could have. As our eyes met, I returned the smile, secure in knowing his reciprocal affection. Our bond was extraordinary and deeply rooted in trust, loyalty, and mutual respect. I waved goodbye and headed toward the pen, brushing off the strange feeling that had crept into my mind.

8

BOBBI-CAT

AS I MEANDERED, searching for Cody, I spotted Felicia, the Turkish Angora cat, charming him by the "sideshow" tent. Her irresistible allure drew my attention, and a twinge of envy pricked my heart. She was the star of the acrobatic cat act, her beauty and flexibility consistently stunning the audience.

Felicia's trim waist and full hips perfectly accentuated her curves, lending her an elegant and seductive appearance. Her white coat was soft and alluring, further enhancing her appeal.

49

Hiding behind the ticket booth, I peeked out, my heart sinking at the sight of Felicia brushing up against Cody. The way she laughed and flirted churned my stomach with unease.

Felicia had a string of boyfriends, so I couldn't comprehend why she needed to captivate Cody's attention. As I questioned her actions, the realization hit me like a ton of bricks. During our grooming session, I had confided in her about my feelings for Cody. I found her friendly and genuine, never suspecting her intentions to be less than sincere.

Glancing in Cody's direction, my heart fluttered at the sight of his stunning and refined features. He possessed an extraordinary level of handsomeness with his sleek, long hair. The tufts of fur on his ears and paws only enhanced his rugged and attractive appearance. His sturdy shoulders and brawny chest emanated a sense of vigor and force. The sheer power of his magnetism and charisma was impossible to resist, leaving me entirely captivated and entranced.

As Felicia leaned forward and kissed him, my heart sank with disappointment.

Cody stepped back in surprise.

"What are you doing?" he murmured, unsure how to react to her sudden advances.

"Do I frighten you?" she asked.

Puffing out his chest, Cody replied, "No... I was just surprised you kissed me. I wasn't expecting it."

"Don't you find me pretty?" she asked, fluttering her eyelashes seductively.

Cody seemed uneasy as he took another step back, but she kept moving closer, complimenting his attractive features and hinting that girls were competing for his attention. Her words stung deeply, especially when she included me in the list of admirers.

To my surprise, Cody said he knew and liked me.

His words upset Felicia, who commented about me being "moggy."

"I disagree. I find her attractive."

My heart skipped a beat, hearing him defend me.

"We're performers. She's nothing but a rat killer," Felicia retorted.

"Everyone knows that's not true, except for the ringmaster. She's not capable of killing anything. Sofia feeds her," Cody responded sternly.

"Interesting," Felicia murmured, with a smile tugging at the corners of her lips. Without hesitation, she continued, "You'd lower your standards for her?"

Cody scowled and retorted, "Standards? Bobbi-Cat is the most affectionate feline here. Just because she isn't a circus performer doesn't mean she's inferior to us."

"I disagree," she retorted.

"Your negative attitude is unappealing. Your jealousy is unsettling," Cody replied.

Taken aback by his comment, Felicia stepped back in shock. Struggling to formulate an appropriate response, she trailed off, unable to find the right words.

Cody found Felicia's response amusing. "Has no one been honest with you before?"

She let out a loud huff and continued to walk away with determined steps. Hoping to catch Cody's attention, she exaggerated the swing of her hips a little more than usual.

Nonetheless, he remained disinterested, shaking his head while feeling embarrassed for her.

My presence became known as I stepped out from my hiding spot. Cody turned around and greeted me with a warm smile. He asked if I had heard what had transpired.

I nodded in affirmation.

"The audacity of her..." he muttered under his breath.

"I never realized you had feelings for me," I confessed bashfully.

"I can't keep my eyes off of you!"

A smile spread across my face as I gently brushed against him. The deep, rhythmic purring that resonated from his chest solidified the bond of our friendship. His robust body leaned back against mine, causing a sudden surge of excitement to rush through me. It was as if a swarm of butterflies had taken flight within me. The allure of his muscular physique left me slightly dizzy, and his presence enthralled my senses.

"Where are you headed?"

"I'm just going for a walk. Taking in the evening," I replied, slightly out of breath.

He responded quickly—his voice tinged with interest. "May I join you? It would be an excellent opportunity for us to get acquainted."

A nod of agreement came quickly, my excitement clear. As we began our stroll, an unexpected commotion caught our attention. We turned in unison to witness Felicia darting away. A shared sense of concern and confusion washed over us, her erratic behavior leaving us puzzled.

Cody broke the silence, his voice laced with worry. "She's capable of terrible things," he cautioned. Deep lines of worry etched onto his face as he added, "I'd advise you to keep your distance."

Understanding dawned upon me as I nodded in acknowledgment, aware of Felicia's potential for trouble. Our steps fell in sync once more as we resumed our walk, the unsettling incident fading into the background.

My thoughts slowly meandered back to Cody, his presence comforting. After a while, I stopped in my tracks, turning toward him. With a boldness that surprised me, I leaned in and kissed him. His initial surprise swiftly transformed into pure delight as he returned the kiss with equal fervor. Once the moment passed, he looked at me with a hopeful gleam.

"Will you watch my performance tomorrow?"

Without hesitation, I responded with bubbling enthusiasm, "I wouldn't miss it for the world!"

9

SOFIA

A S THE RINGMASTER and I stood before Taya's enclosure, I felt saddened by the sign that announced, "The Only Baby Amur Leopard on Earth." Instinctively, I asked the carnies to adjust the banner to the right to ensure proper alignment on the cage.

"Alert the news stations!" Philip commanded, fulfilling his role as the leader. "Inform them about the newborn," he added, taking a step back to assess the sign's positioning.

I nodded as Billy-Joe attached the sign to the wooden exterior of the cage. Soon after, I noticed a sly grin spreading across Sam's face as he winked at Billy-Joe. Their shared laughter caused Billy-Joe to lose his grip on the hammer, sending it tumbling to the ground.

The noise drew the ringmaster's ire.

"Pay attention to what you're doing! You could hurt someone!" he bellowed.

"Yes, sir," Billy-Joe mumbled, glancing at Sam, who was still wearing an amused grin.

Unseen by Philip, Sam silently whispered to Billy-Joe, "We'll do it tonight." This cryptic message, with an unclear meaning, stirred a sense of unease.

After the ringmaster departed, I crouched down and began petting Chief at my feet. He was a handsome boy, loyal to his mate, and a trustworthy companion. He immediately smiled as I kissed him on the forehead, feeling my love for him. "You're such a good boy," I said as he softly barked and looked toward Taya and her baby, showing his protective presence.

The carnies stepped away without a word, leaving me with an odd feeling in the pit of my stomach again—something wasn't quite right.

Upon hearing Taya roar from her cage—thanking me for my help—a warm smile covered my face, understanding the joy shared between a mother and her baby.

"I'm so happy for you," I whispered, reaching forward and gently petting the little cub's head.

Mischa meowed softly, approving of my friendship.

I bid everyone goodnight and walked through the circus grounds, greeting each animal I passed to ensure their safety and contentment. My heart ached for the animals—prisoners confined within cages. Despite the ringmaster's contrasting view, I did everything possible to make them feel loved and secure. He regarded them merely as performers—seeing how he treated these gentle beings broke my heart.

Turning around, I heard Bobbi-Cat running toward me to catch up. Bending down, I lifted her into my arms, and she meowed enthusiastically. Smiling, I asked, "What's gotten you so excited?"

She meowed again.

Something wonderful had occurred, and she was eager to share it. Wishing I could understand, I kissed her belly and pretended to listen.

Upon reaching my quaint, somewhat weather-beaten trailer, I stepped inside, leaving the door slightly ajar for Molly—anticipating she'd join us for the night. Gently, I placed Bobbi-Cat down, immediately feeling the soothing blast of air from the air conditioner, a blissful relief from the day's fatigue. In the quiet of my trailer, I began boiling water for tea.

As the water simmered, I tended to Bobbi-Cat, feeding her with the gentle care that had become a cherished routine for both of us. She reciprocated in the sincerest way she knew, nuzzling against my legs and purring with contentment.

I then undressed, shedding the layers of my day and its burdens. With a steaming cup, I crawled into bed, the comfort of its familiar, enveloping warmth greeting me like an old friend. No sooner had I settled in than Bobbi-Cat jumped up and cuddled beside me.

Her purring filled the room as I relaxed, stroking her with gentle, rhythmic motions. It eased my loneliness and anxious heart, reminding me that tomorrow would bring another day—a never-ending cycle of responsibilities.

10

MADDIE

WITH A SLOW and measured pace, I began my journey toward Taya's cage to bid Chief goodnight. My belly, heavy and extended because of the advanced stages of pregnancy, made the walk more taxing than usual. I should have opted to stay within the confines of my kennel, but the desire to see my husband outweighed my physical discomfort. His duty of standing guard over Taya had encroached upon our time, which weighed heavily on our hearts.

I was aware of his guilt for our inability to spend quality time together. But we were bound by the stringent rules imposed by the ringmaster. Any deviation could cause severe consequences—being cast out onto the streets or sent to an animal shelter. To ease his guilt, I reassured him I understood our predicament. Yet, despite my words of comfort, I knew it pained him to be away from me.

Despite the challenging conditions, I swelled with pride. Chief showed complete devotion to his duties. It was clear to all who observed him he derived great satisfaction and honor from his work.

A tender smile played on my lips as my thoughts meandered toward our unborn pup. Chief and I were reddish-golden retrievers, our fur boasting a distinct reddish-orange hue. There was little doubt in my mind that our baby would inherit his father's striking appearance. Carrying just one pup instead of a litter was perplexing, but I didn't let it bother me. Instead, my heart swelled with immense gratitude and joy at the impending arrival of motherhood.

As I neared Taya's cage, Chief's attention shifted toward me. The stern, protective expression etched onto his face softened, making way for a warm, welcoming smile.

"You shouldn't have come," he gently admonished.

"I know," I acknowledged, "But I needed to see you before I went to bed."

Rising from his spot, Chief approached me. He tenderly kissed my forehead before enveloping me in a comforting embrace as I settled beside him. I took a deep breath, letting his love and warmth wash over me. As he pulled away, he held my gaze, his eyes overflowing with adoration.

"You're so beautiful!" he murmured.

His words, though heartfelt, felt foreign to me. With my swollen belly and the various discomforts that accompanied pregnancy, feeling beautiful seemed a distant reality.

"The love you radiate is astounding. Motherhood truly becomes you," he added, his voice filled with awe.

Lifting my head, I returned his affection with a gentle kiss. His soft moan echoed my feelings of love for him. "I love you," I confessed.

Once more, Chief held me close, and our shared love enveloped the silence. After a few moments, he cast a concerned glance, advising me to get some rest. His words resonated with my feelings, the pain from my swollen belly growing increasingly persistent. I knew it was time to lie down.

"Do you need help back?" he asked.

I acknowledged his concern with a shake of my head. "I'll be fine," I said, my gaze lingering on his face. A sharp intake of breath slipped past my lips as I admired his handsome features, feeling an overwhelming sense of pride for having him as the father of my baby.

"Goodnight," I murmured softly.

"Be careful going back," he cautioned, his protective instincts never failing to surface.

"I will," I reassured him.

The journey back to the kennel was a challenge in my condition, but I navigated my way. Being confined within the cage overnight was daunting, often leading to long, restless nights. Thankfully, Sofia, the ever-so-caring ring mistress, always left my cage unlocked, allowing me the freedom to step out if needed. Sofia was another blessing in my life. Her constant love and guidance have been invaluable throughout my pregnancy. It was as if she inherently understood the trials and tribulations of motherhood.

Turning in circles until the urge to settle down overpowered me, I nestled into the straw-laden floor of my cage. The straw seemed to envelop me, wrapping me in a cocoon of warmth and love. Slowly, I lowered my head onto the straw, my eyes slipping closed as exhaustion took hold. Soon, I drifted into a deep sleep, my dreams filled with images of my soon-to-be-born little boy.

11

SAM

A S THE SYMPHONY of crickets filled the air, I moved forward stealthily, swinging the bat lightly to keep my muscles loose. Billy-Joe trailed behind me, his heart heavy with remorse for our grim task—stealing Taya and Mischa.

Every step was a gamble, a heart-pounding bet on silence. As we rounded the corner, Chief came into view, sprawled out on the ground, lost in a deep slumber. His loyalty to the leopards was evident, even in repose, his massive frame a silent sentinel.

My eyes locked onto the cage that held Taya and Mischa, their forms barely discernible in the dim light, their gentle breaths the only sign of life. Eager to keep the peace of the moment undisturbed, I raised a finger to my lips, eyes wide with caution, signaling Billy-Joe to maintain absolute silence. Each second stretched into an eternity, the weight of our mission bearing down on us.

We began inching toward the truck, each footfall deliberate and soundless. As I outstretched my hand to grasp the door handle, Chief's eyes snapped open abruptly, shattering his peaceful slumber. By a stroke of luck, I sidestepped a confrontation with him. Reacting swiftly, I vaulted into the truck. Billy-Joe, however, was not as fortunate and found himself at the receiving end of Chief's wrath

Chief lunged at him, sinking his teeth into his leg. The sudden attack elicited a sharp cry of pain from Billy-Joe, piercing the night air.

Adrenaline coursed through me, fueling my instinct to protect my friend. Without a second thought, I sprang out of the truck, baseball bat clutched firmly in my grasp, ready to stand against Chief in defense of Billy-Joe.

Chief groaned in pain and staggered backward, eyes blazing with fury from my hit. Instantly, he was back on his feet, charging aggressively toward me. His jaws dripped with drool as he lunged, baring his snarling teeth. Despite being evenly matched, I had to fight with all my might as we clashed violently. His heavy breathing and snarls echoed through the air as we circled each other. For every bat swing, Chief countered with fierce bites and clawing paws. Sweat poured down my face, stinging my eyes and blurring my vision.

As the battle waged on, I could feel my strength ebbing away. But I took a deep breath, raised the bat one last time, and swung it down with all my might. With a sickening thud, Chief's body slumped to the ground as the bat hit him. My heart pounded in my chest. I stood there, afraid but relieved that the ordeal was over.

Billy-Joe pointed in shock at Chief's motionless form and started sobbing loudly. "You've killed him!" he exclaimed, disbelief and horror etched into his words.

I stood over Chief, consumed by a heavy feeling of guilt. No matter how much I wished I could undo what had been done, it was too late.

I took a deep breath and shouted at Billy-Joe to get in the truck. Still sobbing and shaking, he obeyed my orders.

I lifted my gaze and saw Axle barreling toward me, drawn by Chief's cries. My heart pounded with fear and fury, emotions swirling like a storm. Gripping the bat tighter, my arms quivered with adrenaline coursing through my veins. I steeled myself, bracing for the impending confrontation.

Axle lunged at me, his jaws snapping at my face. I dodged his blows, swinging the bat with all my might. It connected with his shoulder, making him stumble backward. But he didn't give up. He kept coming at me, his movements fueled by fierce determination.

The battle between us was intense and heart-wrenching as we exchanged bites and blows. Blood dripped from our wounds, staining the ground beneath us.

At one point, Axle disarmed me, snatching the bat out of my grip. But I refused to back down. I charged and tackled him.

Gaining the upper hand, I landed a final blow with my fist on Axle's head. He crumpled, defeated. Wasting no time, I hopped in the truck, and we drove away from the scene.

As I glanced in the rearview mirror, I saw Chief's lifeless body and Axle standing above him, weeping inconsolably.

12

MARCEAU

THE COLORFUL SIGHTS overwhelmed Molly and me as we walked along the circus midway. At one point, I directed her attention to a truck's sign. Although the vehicle was clearly past its prime, with its chipping paint and faded appearance, its sign remained just as captivating as ever.

The painting vividly illustrated my mother, captured mid-leap through a flaming hoop, in a spectacular circus act. The painting also depicted my father, the other dog, balancing a spinning ball on his snout, highlighting the contrast between his muscular form and my mother's slender frame. The painter depicted both with such attention to detail that they seemed almost lifelike. He rendered their fur in delicate brushstrokes and made their eyes gleam with intelligence and spirit.

"My parents were famous circus performers," I began, my voice filled with pride and nostalgia. As I spoke, Molly's gaze drifted toward the painting of my father, his face mirroring mine in a striking resemblance that was impossible to overlook. His eyes, the same deep shade of brown as mine, twinkled with mirth and mischief, while his strong jawline and high cheekbones were traits I had inherited.

My heart raced as she leaned into me, and warmth spread through my body. Without thinking, I leaned forward and kissed her. She sighed, wanting the kiss just as badly as I did. The electricity of our attraction was unmistakable. As we continued to kiss, I felt an intense heat in my chest, which seemed to grow with each passing moment.

When we broke apart, we stared into each other's eyes, seemingly unable to look away. A thousand unsaid words seemed to hang between us. All that mattered at that moment was the mutual understanding that this connection was real and precious beyond measure.

As if on cue, I leaned in closer as we admired the painting of my parents in silence. After a moment, I turned and asked if she wanted to grab something to eat. Despite knowing the baker was busy getting ready for tomorrow's breakfast, I was confident he would offer us a treat despite being strictly forbidden to do so.

"I would like that!" Molly replied eagerly.

As we walked toward the dining tent, I confided I had never been in love before. She listened attentively as I did my best to describe my life up to this point. In turn, she shared her story of the terrifying storm that separated her from her human companion. When I asked about her past romantic relationships, she shook her head and admitted that she was waiting for the right one.

I thought about wanting to experience love for myself. As much as I cherished my friends and their companionship, I knew it was time to explore a different aspect of life. I could sense that Molly felt the same way, too, and I found comfort in knowing I wasn't alone.

Entering the kitchen tent, I barked at the baker. He stopped what he was doing, understanding we were looking for a treat.

"Young lovers!" he exclaimed, raising his hand in an Italian gesture. "Sit! I'll bring you a treat!" He elaborated in his foreign accent.

We sat down, and he placed a freshly baked cinnamon roll between us. The treat was a sight to behold—a golden spiral of fluffy dough laced with warm hues of cinnamon. It had a velvety frosting that glistened in the tent's soft lighting, tempting us with its irresistible decadence. The scent wafting from it was intoxicating, making our mouths water in anticipation. It was warm to the touch, and as we pulled apart the spiraled layers, steam rose, carrying an even stronger burst of heavenly aroma.

While savoring the mouthwatering treat, my thoughts turned toward Molly and the future we might share. The idea of her being my partner and starting a family filled me with excitement that rivaled the sweetness of our shared dessert. The thought of being a father to our future puppies filled my heart with joy and anticipation.

Suddenly, a mournful howl pierced the air, shattering our peaceful moment. It was Axle. The sound was gut-wrenching, filled with despair and anguish. It echoed through the stillness, hanging heavy in the air long after it had ceased. It was a sound that sent chills down my spine, a sound no one ever wanted to hear.

Molly and I locked eyes without speaking, and mutual understanding passed between us. Together, we bolted from the tent. Our steps were swift, gravel crunching under our paws as we sprinted toward him.

13

AXLE

THE SCENE BEFORE ME was devastating, a sight that made my heart sink with sorrow. Chief's body lay on the ground, his once vibrant form still and lifeless. His coat, usually glossy and brimming with life, seemed dull under the harsh midway light. His eyes, always filled with a playful spark, were closed, their twinkle forever extinguished.

I stooped down to nuzzle him, hoping for a reaction, a sign that this was all some terrible mistake. But there was none. His body was cold and unresponsive, contrasting with the warmth and love he had always radiated. Caught in a dilemma, I stood frozen, torn between the instinct to chase after the truck and save Taya and Mischa or stay by my friend's side. My heart pounded painfully in my chest, each beat echoing the loss that I was feeling.

An overwhelming wave of despair washed over me, pulling me under its dark, unforgiving tide. I let out a mournful howl, a raw and primal expression of my agony. It was a sound that echoed through the stillness, marking the moment of an irreplaceable loss.

I sank to the ground, cradling Chief's lifeless body against my heaving chest. My tears fell freely, each droplet a testament to my sorrow, staining the earth beneath us.

The world around me blurred as if smudged by my tears. I clung to my best friend, my companion, my confidante, mourning his loss. His absence was a gaping hole, a void that nothing could fill.

Marceau and Molly arrived, hearing my mournful howl. Their shocked gasps filled the air as they tried to comprehend what had happened.

Hearing the fleeing truck backfire, Marceau looked up and, without hesitation, charged forward upon hearing Taya's distress call, barking in pursuit.

As the tears continued to flow freely from my eyes, Molly stepped forward, whimpering in empathy but not knowing what to do. The thought of Chief's wife and unborn baby filled me with grief, and my sobs grew even louder as I wept for them.

14

SAM

MY EXCITEMENT WAS CLEAR, and I couldn't help but slam my hand down on the steering wheel, exclaiming, "We're going to be rich!" However, Billy-Joe was still mourning Chief's passing, wiping away tears. Desperate to lift his spirits, I repeated my statement, nudging his shoulder in hopes he'd share my enthusiasm.

Glancing in the rearview mirror, I saw Marceau chasing the truck. In an unexpected move, the little dog lunged forward, scrambling onto the back of the vehicle, his hind legs trailing behind. Feeling a surge of mischief, I stepped on the gas pedal. Hitting a bump, the dog lost his grip and tumbled in a cloud of dust.

"Who's buying Taya and Mischa?" Billy-Joe finally asked, breaking his silence.

"A furrier," I replied.

Billy-Joe's jaw dropped in shock.

"How else are we going to make money?" I asked, shaking my head at his sensitivity. "The ringmaster gets what's coming to him..." With that, I exited the circus grounds and drove toward the marshlands of Audubon Park.

"He'll kill them," Billy-Joe murmured.

As I drove, a wave of overwhelming remorse swept over me. I didn't want to reveal my weakness or show any vulnerability. Despite anticipating a new life, I couldn't shake the memory of taking Chief's life and soon, Taya's and Mischa's. Thinking of Chief's unborn pup, my heart broke at the idea of him growing up without ever knowing his father. I forced myself to stop, shaking the thoughts from my head. I refused to feel responsible for the suffering of these animals, reminding myself that the ringmaster had this coming to him. Seeking a distraction from my grief, I turned to Billy-Joe, suggesting he could buy that above-ground swimming pool he always wanted.

He opened his mouth to reply, but all that came out was a shuddering cry.

I noticed the gaps where teeth should have been. I realized my mistake—I should have suggested he fix his teeth instead of buying a swimming pool. However, I held my tongue, figuring it would worsen the situation.

Suddenly, the rearview mirror caught my attention. The sign emblazoned with "The Only Baby Amur Leopard on Earth" detached itself from Taya's cage with a sudden jerk. It seemed to hover in the air momentarily as though suspended in time before it began its descent. As it tumbled through the air, spinning and twirling, it painted a surreal picture against the backdrop of the night sky.

When it finally hit the ground, it skidded across the asphalt, raising a small cloud of dust. The sight of the sign flying off the truck and landing motionless on the street was like a punch to the gut. It was a stark reminder of Chief's life, now just as still and silent as the discarded sign.

I realized then that I had been holding my breath, the tension in my body mirroring the turmoil within me. Seeing the sign lying motionless on the ground cemented the finality of Chief's passing.

With a heavy sigh, I took a deep breath, once again pushing the guilt and sorrow away. I had to keep moving forward for myself and the promise of better days.

15

MORTON

AS MY HEAD popped out from beneath the straw-covered cage floor, the rhythmic rumbling of the truck vibrated through my chest. The world outside transformed into a dizzying blur of colors and shapes, leaving me utterly bewildered. Turning to Taya, I asked, "Why is the truck moving?"

"We've been kidnapped."

Her words hit me like a ton of bricks. My shock quickly morphed into a suffocating wave of panic, threatening to drag me under.

"Stay calm..." She murmured.

Panic devoured me. My heart raced, and my breath quickened. In a grand display, I flung myself onto the floor and wailed, "We're doomed! DOOMED!"

"Oh, Morton..." Taya sighed.

I launched into a feverish monologue about all the creative and horrifying ways we might meet our end, each scenario more outrageous than the last.

"Morton, please!"

I couldn't help but spiral deeper into my overactive imagination. The more I rambled, the more terrified I became.

"Please, stop!"

I gasped, dramatically clutching my paw to my chest as the weight of my foolishness crashed down on me. "I don't know what I was thinking," I admitted, my voice trembling. "I'm sorry! The pressure of being kidnapped... IS JUST TOO OVERWHELMING!"

"Lie down and relax," she suggested.

I nodded and settled beside her, paralyzed by the magnitude of our situation. Calming down, I realized that my imagination had only amplified my fear.

However, my newfound stillness was short-lived. The truck's brakes screeched with a horrific, ear-splitting shriek, and we came to a bone-rattling stop. In an instant, my serenity shattered—again. Fear surged through me, and I leaped up, flailing like a fish out of water.

At this point, Taya lost her composed demeanor and became frightened. She stood up, her voice cutting through my panic as tears spilled down her cheeks.

"Morton, you must do something! Save my baby!"

Her cries engulfed me in a suffocating wave of dread, pushing me closer to the brink of collapse. It was as if the weight of the world rested on my shoulders. "I—I don't know what to do!" I stammered, struggling to think straight.

"Get Axle!" Taya shouted, her plea piercing through my fog of terror.

The thought of running back to the circus grounds felt impossible. My breaths became ragged and shallow, and I doubled over, clutching my chest in despair. In a trembling voice, I protested, "I'm just a mouse!" I felt utterly insignificant, crushed beneath the monumental task before me. My eyes widened, locking onto hers, paralyzed by the moment's weight.

"You're the only one who can save us."

My breath grew even more erratic. I began to hyperventilate.

"Morton... help us..."

Despite the crushing impossibility of it all, a flicker of resolve sparked within me. I sucked in a deep breath, trying to summon the courage I didn't know I had. My heart continued to race as I looked at Taya.

She gave me a nod of encouragement.

I murmured my promise to return and squeezed through the cage bars. Standing on the edge of the flatbed, I looked down into an endless abyss. Fear surged through me. I closed my eyes, trying to calm the storm within. After an eternity, I forced my eyes open, steeling myself for what lay ahead. With a final, shuddering breath, I leaped into the darkness.

The sudden impact jolted my body to its core, sending me tumbling wildly across the ground for several painful seconds. Lying in the darkness, a deep wave of loneliness washed over me. A sniffle escaped my throat. Would anyone miss me if something happened?

A surge of determination filled every part of my being. If I survived this ordeal, I vowed to make drastic changes, starting with becoming friendlier and more open to others. With newfound courage coursing through my veins, I bid farewell to Taya.

Above me, shrouded in the darkness of night, an owl let out a hoot. Its eerie call made me halt. As I gathered my courage and pressed on, Taya unexpectedly bellowed back, catching me completely off guard. I stopped again to listen but failed to understand her.

Carefully taking another step, I extended my paws to navigate the enveloping darkness. The thought of unseen horrors lurking just out of sight sent waves of chills through me, leaving me quaking with apprehension. Suddenly, a match flared, igniting a campfire. I turned to see two silhouetted figures—Sam and Billy-Joe, the circus carnies.

Panicking, I quickly searched for something that could serve as a weapon. As my gaze fell upon a nearby stick, I eagerly grabbed it, ready to use it. However, my body trembled uncontrollably with fear, so much so that the stick tumbled from my grasp and clattered to the ground. At that moment, I truly understood just how hopelessly outmatched I was by these two men.

16

ELSA

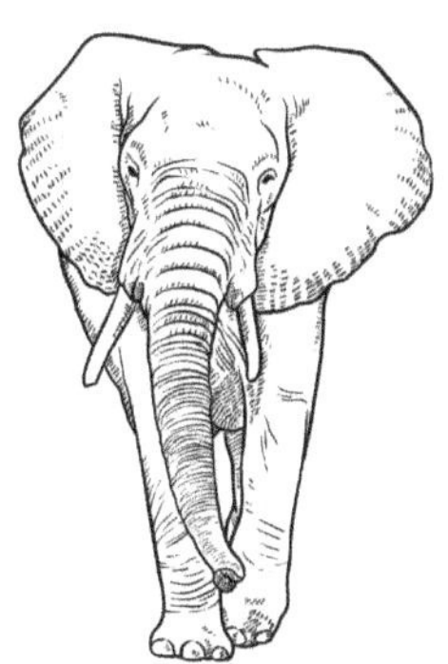

A S AXLE'S DISTRESS CRIES echoed in the distance—I tugged violently on the chain binding me. Across the midway, Axle and Sofia stood over Chief's body, their faces filled with grief. In stark contrast, the ringmaster stood, showing no sorrow, only frustration. The loss of Taya and Mischa had hit him hard financially.

My mother stepped forward and held me—her trunk radiating an infinite warmth of love.

"Everything will be okay," she murmured into my ear, trying to offer a glimmer of hope amidst all the darkness that surrounded us.

My gaze drifted toward Axle again, and my heart broke as he lifted his head and let out a sorrowful howl—a sound of utter grief that only a best friend could understand. I raised my trunk to the sky in response, sending a mourning call. His voice echoed back with pain and longing. The sheer suffering was too much to bear, so I redoubled my efforts to break free from the chain that held me in place.

My mother objected frantically, warning that the ringmaster would punish me for this act of defiance. But I refused to listen, knowing Axle needed me. I fought against the chain with all my might until I finally dislodged the stake from the earth. With one final heave, freedom was mine. I turned around to leave, but my mother grabbed my tail and stopped me.

"Elsa, no..." she pleaded desperately—her voice full of worry for my safety.

"Axle needs me," I appealed.

Sofia looked up and noticed something was amiss. She excused herself from Philip Andrews and headed toward us. As sobs escaped my mouth, she quickly realized that although I had broken free from the stake, I was not intending to run away.

"Oh, Elsa," she said, embracing me.

My mother joined us, raising her trunk and enveloping us in boundless love and understanding. No words could convey the turmoil in my heart, so all I could do was weep uncontrollably while leaning on them.

With no need to be told the reason for my tears, Sofia instinctively understood they were for Axle.

"I'm worried about him, too," she said.

From the moment I was born, Axle had been a parental figure. I had a father, but he belonged to a different circus, and I had no idea where he was.

My mother met him when we joined the "Ultimate Circus Extravaganza" in Chicago, Illinois, where two circuses came together under one roof. After performing an act together, they fell in love.

When Sofia learned of my mother's pregnancy, she contacted the circus' ringmaster, but he was as inauspicious as ours and wouldn't release him.

Whenever I feel sad about not knowing my father, my mother comforts me by sharing vivid stories of their time together.

Sofia's tender kiss on my forehead quelled the inner turmoil inside me.

"Elsa," Sofia whispered, "Stay here with your mother, and don't leave her side. Don't worry about the stake. I'll fix it, and the ringmaster won't suspect anything."

"Thank you," I trumpeted.

Sofia assured me she would take Axle to the medical tent for treatment.

As Sofia walked away, my heart weighed down with sorrow. I had never experienced such excruciating pain before.

"You need to help Axle tomorrow. He won't be able to oversee everyone..." my mother murmured to me.

"I'll help him," I promised. Glancing back across the midway, I saw the ringmaster carrying Chief away. Another tear escaped my eye when I saw Axle wanting to follow them instead of seeking medical attention. With a heavy heart, Sofia gently led him in the opposite direction.

"Why, Mother?" I wailed.

"Oh, Elsa... I wish I could explain, but life isn't always fair."

My mother's words resonated deeply, and I understood that life could be unpredictable. It made me appreciate the loved ones in my life and cherish every moment with them.

17

SAM

HAVING COLLECTED FIREWOOD and sparked a campfire, I hauled over two logs for us to perch upon. We had found sanctuary away from the flatbed truck, yet the distant cries of Taya and Mischa still echoed hauntingly. After all the evening's excitement, we had to unwind.

I delved into my pocket, pulling out a metallic flask. The campfire's glow caused the metal to shimmer in the enveloping darkness. Unscrewing the cap, I took a hearty gulp, relishing the smooth flavor of whiskey. As my companion reached for the container, I playfully chided him to wait his turn. After quenching my thirst, I passed it to him.

Out of the corner of my eye, I caught sight of a plump mouse perched at the edge of the campsite. With a watchful gaze fixed upon us, it assessed our every move. As my eyes locked in an unexpected moment of connection, the mouse shuddered with fear and quickly hurried away into the darkness.

A shiver coursed through my body, my deep-seated phobia of rodents rearing its ugly head. I turned my attention back to Billy-Joe just in time to witness him raising the flask to his lips again.

Reacting quickly, I snatched it from his grip and, to my dismay, realized it was now empty.

"You drank it all!" I exclaimed, dismayed at the prospect of a long night ahead without a single drop of liquid refreshment.

Billy-Joe gave me a toothless grin.

"You muttonhead!" I shouted, hitting him with my trusty baseball cap. "Where's your flask?"

"Inside the glove compartment," he murmured, covering his head.

Taking a deep breath to steady my nerves, I stood and lifted my cap to deliver another blow but halted midway. He screamed for me to stop, and I gave him an exasperated look before walking toward the truck.

As I approached the vehicle, the heavy-set mouse again caught my attention. Its beady eyes were wide with fright, and I could sense its unease as it stood frozen in its tracks.

The mouse and I let out a simultaneous scream, and it scurried away in the opposite direction. I took a deep breath, trying to gather my composure, wondering why I feared the tiny creature so much.

Resuming my task, I retrieved the flask.

Exiting the truck, I scanned my surroundings. My eyes caught sight of the mouse scurrying underneath the vehicle. I hesitated momentarily, then jumped forward to scare it, chuckling at my foolishness.

Dismissing the rodent from my mind, I returned to the campsite. I lifted the flask toward Billy-Joe, and he looked up upon my return.

Anticipating the refreshing contents, he reached for it eagerly, but I pulled it away just in time.

"Not so fast, little buddy," I said, gesturing toward the mouse that had returned to the edge of the campsite.

As Billy-Joe caught sight of the rodent, he uttered an unexpected high-pitched scream, startling the little creature. It darted off into the night. After the initial fright had passed, Billy-Joe couldn't help but chuckle at his overreaction.

"A grown man afraid of a mouse!" he exclaimed between fits of laughter.

We laughed and shared a moment of understanding as we passed the flask back and forth. The crackling of the fire grew louder, and its amber glow cast a warm and comforting light on our moment of refuge. We could forget about Taya and her baby for just a few moments until their sorrowful cries once again echoed in the background.

But for now, we sat in silence, enjoying each other's company and the peacefulness of the night. The stars twinkled above us, and the breeze carried the scent of wild jasmine. It was a moment of respite from the chaos of circus life.

18

LUCA

T HE DISTANT HOWLING filled me with unease and confusion as I lay in the darkness. Axle had left in a rush, responding to Chief's call for help while urging me to stay in the pen. An overwhelming sense of helplessness and abandonment took hold, making my heart race.

As my fears intensified, memories of my mother came flooding back, and I couldn't help but feel the wrenching pain of being separated from her. A tear slid down my cheek, and I hastily wiped it away with my hoof, trying to maintain my composure.

In the pitch-blackness, I longed for the comfort of Axle's presence. The distant howling only heightened my fear, and I couldn't shake the feeling that something was wrong.

After what felt like a very long time, a sudden noise broke the silence behind me. I turned around and saw Axel and Sofia standing at the pen's entrance. My confusion grew as she urged him to rest. As Sofia left and Axel approached me, my heart swelled with emotion, and the floodgates of tears broke open.

I could no longer hold back the sobs as the overwhelming fear of being alone in the darkness gripped me. The aching thought of my mother intensified my grief.

"I've been so scared!" I cried

"Don't be afraid. I'm here now." Axle replied, trying to reassure me.

"Why was I taken from my mother?" I pressed—confusion evident in my voice.

Axle sighed deeply before answering with tenderness, "For reasons you would never understand."

My mind raced with questions. "Did I do something wrong?"

"No, Luca... It was all for monetary reasons."

Unsure of what he meant, I asked, "What does that mean?"

"They sold you for money."

My heart sank as I absorbed the truth. "Oh," I breathed, struggling to comprehend how anyone could tear a mother and baby apart. "Where is she?" I asked, my voice trembling with desperation.

"She's at the New Orleans Zoo."

I felt a pang of sadness and lowered my head, unable to find words. The weight of the situation left me speechless.

After a long silence, I listened as Axle shared the harrowing news of Taya and Mischa's kidnapping, as well as the passing of Chief. Shocked, I turned toward him and noticed the bandages wrapped around his legs, filling me with concern over the extent of the situation.

"Th-they hurt you too," I said, my voice trembling with sadness.

Axel bowed his head, tears in his eyes. "He was my best friend," he confessed, his voice thick with grief.

His words resonated deeply, and my heart ached for his pain. I instinctively reached out my hoof, offering comfort.

As silence settled between us once more, my thoughts drifted to death, a mystery filled with so many unanswered questions. Turning to Axle, I asked, "What happens after we die?"

He remained quiet, lost in thought.

"Axle?"

"I honestly don't know."

"Oh..." I replied, grappling with the depth of his uncertainty.

"No one knows..."

Listening to Axle speak of Chief, the tremble in his voice revealed a love deeper than friendship. My eyes started to water, not from judgment, but from understanding. As I listened to his endearing words, the moonlight broke through the clouds unexpectedly. Axle stopped talking, and we both looked up in surprise. The moonlight's warmth enveloped us, bringing a sense of peace.

As I looked at Axle, his face was a mixture of awe and wonder.

"It's Chief!" I exclaimed, the realization bursting forth like a firecracker. "He's telling us not to worry!"

Axle's eyes glistened with tears of joy.

"He's saying goodbye..." I declared.

As the moonlight shifted behind the clouds, I snuggled with Axle, relishing his warmth and affection. Thinking deeply, I realized that even though Chief had departed this world, he hadn't left us. He'd live on forever in our memories.

19

MORTON

I SCAMPERED AWAY from the campsite, clumsily navigating the rough terrain with my paws. En route to the bridge over the lagoon, a spooky, elongated "hooooooo" echoed through the night. It sent shivers down my spine and prompted me to quicken my pace.

Shortly after, two more haunting hoots reverberated above me. Sensing something amiss, I stopped dead in my tracks and looked upward. My breath hitched in my throat as I spotted an owl perched on a branch. Its eyes glowed chillingly, fixed upon me.

Suddenly, with a silent grace that belied its deadly intent, it swooped down, and I realized with a heart-stopping jolt that I was its intended prey. In a moment of pure panic, I squeaked—a pitiful sound of fear—and somersaulted into a nearby thicket of grass to dodge its talons.

I stayed hidden, my tiny heart pounding against my ribcage, until the coast seemed clear. "Goodness gracious," I murmured, the words barely a whisper. I was relieved to have escaped capture. After catching my breath, I peered out, my eyes darting around frantically for any signs of danger. Not seeing the owl, I resumed my scamper down the path.

However, my relief was short-lived. The foreboding figure reappeared, casting a monstrous shadow that wrapped around me like a cloak of dread. In the blink of an eye, the massive owl swooped down with terrifying speed, its wings producing a thunderous rush of air that sent my heart racing. Before I could process what was happening, I felt its razor-sharp claws grip me tightly!

"AHHHHHHH!" I screamed at the top of my lungs. "SOMEBODY HELP ME!" I shrieked, flailing my paws in a panic.

The owl carried me high above the ground.

Filled with visions of my impending doom, an electrifying surge of terror paralyzed my body. Just then, a sudden gust of wind jolted the owl, causing it to wobble awkwardly. My stomach lurched, spiraling violently like a rollercoaster hurtling down its most treacherous slope! With a high-pitched shriek, I flailed my paws frantically in every direction. "Oh, my stars! This can't be happening!" I wailed—my eyes wide with panic as a wave of vertigo crashed over me.

I closed my eyes tightly.

"Calm down! Breathe!" I chanted until the frantic pounding of my heart began to still.

Cautiously, I opened my eyes, only to find the owl gliding serenely through the air, utterly unfazed by my overdramatic display. Looking down, everything appeared like a miniature replica of the world I knew.

"Oh, woe is me!" I sniffled, my whiskers quivering with despair. I looked up at the owl and cried, "I'm too young to die!"

The owl turned its head, its gaze piercing into mine with an intensity that suggested it was aware of my fear.

"I won't eat you," it uttered. "I'm merely transporting you home."

He was, after all, a creature that thrived on the hunt and lived by the kill. "You're taking me home?" I questioned, skepticism creeping into my voice.

"Yes."

"But how did you know I needed help?" I pressed, still doubtful.

"Taya called to me."

"Oh?" I thought deeply. "I see..." Understanding finally sinking in.

"I'm Ollie, the owl."

At that moment, a wave of relief washed over me, erasing the lines of fear previously etched on my face. I smiled, realizing I wouldn't have to brave the dangerous journey home. "I have your promise... you won't release me, right?"

"I promise," he responded firmly.

Inhaling deeply, I let go of my apprehensions and immersed myself in this extraordinary experience, my fluttering heart settling into a rhythm of newfound hope.

"WEEEEEEE!" I exclaimed, my voice echoing through the vast expanse of the night sky. My legs flailed wildly as I succumbed to the thrill of the moment.

"This is unbelievable! Look at me!" I shouted into the darkness, my voice brimming with exhilaration. "I'M FLYING! I'M FLYING!"

As we soared through the air, my fears evaporated, replaced by excitement and wonder. I felt the wind rushing past my face, and the sensation of flight was indescribable. I couldn't help but burst into song.

"Look at me. I'm flying high, soaring past the clouds in the sky. Stars twinkle as I rush by. I'm flying! I'm flying! The world looks so small, but from here, I can see it all..."

As I continued to sing my joyful song, Ollie swayed back and forth to its rhythm. His eyes sparkled with delight, and a broad smile spread across his face.

"I'm flying! I'm flying! I'm feeling joy, feeling light, journeying through the starry night. This feeling inside is oh so bright. I'll never forget this magical night. I'm flying, I'm flying up so high in this wondrous, endless sky."

As my song ended, Ollie made his descent.

Just as we were about to touch down, he released me.

Letting out a furious screech, I plummeted toward the earth and tumbled uncontrollably for what felt like an eternity before coming to a stop.

Slowly regaining my balance, I dusted myself off and looked up at Ollie with annoyance and disbelief. "Couldn't you have landed me a bit more softly?" I grumbled, my voice quivering with agitation.

However, as soon as Ollie started speaking, a chilling sense of terror quickly replaced all my irritation. The memory of my mission, which I had forgotten amidst the excitement of our flight, flooded back.

"You must find Axle. Save Taya and Mischa!" Ollie cried, his eyes glittering with fierce urgency.

I jumped up and down with unbridled enthusiasm, vigorously waving at Ollie as he flew away. "Thank you! Thank you!" I shouted at the top of my lungs, filled with gratitude.

Ollie tilted his wings back and forth in a graceful farewell, acknowledging my goodbye. As he disappeared into the sky, the first light of dawn began to break, leaving me with a lingering sense of awe.

Still buzzing with excitement and adrenaline, I dashed into the circus grounds, paws pounding against the pavement. As I sprinted, I caught sight of the remains of a half-eaten hotdog lying on the ground. My stomach gurgled with hunger, realizing I hadn't eaten. I knew I couldn't afford to stop and eat because time was of the essence.

"Well… maybe just one bite," I rationalized, unable to resist the temptation. Guiltily, I snatched the hotdog and took one massive, satisfying bite, which led to another bite and another…

SOFIA

WALKING AXLE back to the pen, I instructed him to rest. After leaving him behind, I stifled a yawn with a trembling hand, exhaustion washing over me. The haunting memory of being jolted awake by Chief and Axle's frantic cries lingered in my mind, suffocating and relentless. I took a deep breath, knowing that a task still remained—a heartbreaking duty I couldn't avoid. I had to break the news to Maddie about Chief's passing. The mere thought of it caused my heart to constrict painfully. How does one tell a wife about the loss of her husband? The weight of the impending conversation bore down on me.

When I entered the dog trailer, I was surprised to find everyone awake. My attention immediately turned to Maddie's cage, where she lay nestled beside her newborn pup. She had given birth to little Capo amidst the chaos of the night. A sharp intake of breath escaped me as I kneeled before the cage, my eyes welling up at the sight.

"Oh, he's lovely..." I whispered—my voice laced with an aching longing so profound it seemed to fill the room. The urge to cradle him in my arms was overwhelming, a physical need that tugged at my heartstrings with unparalleled force.

Wiping my eyes, I watched as she gently nudged Capo's rear leg with her snout.

Momentary confusion clouded my mind until the devastating reality dawned on me—Capo's carpal pad was missing. The sight set off a fresh wave of tears.

Maddie barked, her sorrow harmonizing with mine. The tone of her bark told me that in her eyes, he was perfect, deformity and all.

Struggling to find the right words amidst a sea of emotion, I reached forward and tenderly stroked her head. "He's beautiful."

She nodded, a small, understanding smile gracing her face.

As more tears fell from my eyes, I took a deep breath, steeling myself for what was to come. "Maddie... I have something to tell you." The words hung heavy in the air, ominous and foreboding, laden with grief yet unvoiced. Her warm smile faded, replaced instantly by a look of dread as if she already knew the heartbreak that awaited her.

"Chief... has passed," I confessed, my voice barely above a whisper, fragile and breaking under the strain of my heartache. The world seemed to come to a screeching halt, the air around us thickening with the weight of my words. Maddie's reaction was immediate and devastating—the pain etched on her face was a mirror of my own, a shared agony that words could scarcely convey.

"I'm so sorry," I choked out, the words a feeble attempt to bridge the chasm of despair that had opened between us.

Maddie looked at me, her eyes wide and pleading for an explanation. As her tears fell, mirroring my own in their silent testimony of loss, I recounted the night's tragic events. She remained silent, absorbing every word, every painful detail of the story that had irrevocably shattered her world.

21

FELICIA

WITH MY HEART pounding in my chest and adrenaline surging through my veins, I raced toward the ringmaster's trailer. The morning was eerily quiet, with everyone still asleep, exhausted from the evening's events. Upon reaching the door, I knocked forcefully with my right paw to announce my presence. When the ringmaster opened the door in his pajamas, I greeted him with an ominous meow and a cunning grin.

Not waiting for an invitation, I bolted inside the trailer, with the ringmaster trailing behind me in confusion. Despite my best efforts, he seemed unable to comprehend my explanation that Sofia was caring for Bobbi-Cat. Exasperated, I continued to meow incessantly.

When he still could not grasp the situation, I moved toward the door, gesturing outside with urgency. At last, understanding dawned on him. He slipped on his loafers and followed me swiftly.

Upon reaching Sofia's trailer, I jumped onto the windowsill and motioned for him to peek inside. He looked through the glass, first noticing Bobbi-Cat's empty bowl on the floor, then spotting her sleeping soundly in Sofia's bed. Seeing Molly, Bobbi-Cat, and Sofia cuddled together, he sighed deeply while patting my head in gratitude.

"I'll handle this later."

As he thanked me, a triumphant smile spread across my face. I knew my scheme was gradually unfolding. My ambitions were limitless, and I was prepared to do whatever it took to achieve my goals—even if it meant betraying those closest to me.

The ringmaster transported me back to the cat trailer. He cradled me gently to show his appreciation for my help. Our arrival stirred the other felines from their slumber, causing a ripple of curiosity to sweep through the trailer.

As we passed Cody's cage, I couldn't resist flashing a smug smile and a hint of arrogance. He knew I was plotting something, but his suspicions didn't bother me. On the contrary, I reveled in the thrill of outmaneuvering my peers, constantly scheming and strategizing to get what I desired.

Once nestled safely within my cage, the ringmaster told me to rest before my matinee performance. I meowed in response, thanking him. After he left, I drifted into the realm of dreams. I envisioned Bobbi-Cat's impending punishment. In the depths of my slumber, I saw her being banished from the circus, her paws tracing a path along a dusty road, condemned to homelessness once more.

22

JETT

LYING ON MY BELLY, I watched with curious eyes as the circus came to life. It was early morning, and as humans passed my cage heading toward the dining tent, they stretched their limbs and fought off yawns. Among them was a tall man who stood out from the rest. I realized he was the "World's Tallest Man." A veritable giant, my dad had once explained. An array of mouth-watering smells interrupted my train of thought. The aroma of what the humans called coffee, mixed with the scents of scrambled eggs, bacon, and pastries, wafted through the air. Each scent was distinct, yet together, they formed a medley that smelled like nothing else.

Feeling invigorated from a good night's sleep and full of youthful energy, I swiftly stood and pounced on my unsuspecting brother. Surprised, he let out a shriek. His cry pierced the tranquil morning air, causing a few performers to glance in our direction with bemused smiles.

Across the cage, our dad, eating his breakfast, showed me a look of annoyance. His eyebrows furrowed, and a slight frown appeared on his usually jovial face. He gestured for us to quiet down—his mouth full of raw meat.

Determined to show strength, I flashed a confident grin and pinned Harry to the floor.

"Fight back!" my dad murmured to my brother.

"Get off me!" Harry cried.

I sat on his chest.

My mom, looking concerned, said, "Jett, it's too early for this..."

I rose and released Harry, who whimpered, feigning injury. A mischievous smile spread across my face, and I ran across the cage and lunged at my father's leg, still eager to demonstrate my toughness.

Dad indulged me, amused by my youthful antics.

"My son, the mighty lion!" he proclaimed, tousling my short mane.

I turned to look at my father, taking in his impressive physique. His body was compact but packed with power. His teeth and jaws, capable of delivering a fatal blow to any prey, were a testament to his strength. With age, his coat had taken on a yellowish-gold hue, and his shaggy mane, a symbol of his maturity and dominance, flowed long and thick around his neck.

"One day, I'll be as big and strong as you!" I declared, pride resonating in my voice.

My father licked me affectionately.

"Oh, Dad!" I said, wiping my face.

"Abioye?" my mother, Eshe, murmured, pointing toward Harry. "Why are you letting Jett be so rough?" she inquired, a hint of disapproval in her voice.

My dad sighed regretfully.

"I was just playing around!" I explained.

"You're stronger than he is. It would be best if you protected him, not pestered him," my mother instructed.

"Yes," I replied, feeling a sense of shame.

As my father walked over to Harry to give him a nudge, I couldn't help but smile at their interaction. Harry sat up, and my dad playfully licked his face, eliciting a smile. "Have you been practicing your roar?"

My brother shook his head.

My dad then insisted he try. I couldn't resist joining the conversation, giggling as I muttered, "He doesn't know how to do it!"

"That's enough, Jett!"

Harry crouched down and took a deep breath. The sound that he emitted wasn't a roar but a high-pitched squeak. I fell to the straw laughing hysterically as my dad smirked, finding the situation amusing, too.

"Abioye?" my mom muttered in surprise.

My dad cleared his throat to get my attention and shook his head, signaling me to stop laughing. "That's enough, son..."

"Yes, Dad."

"Let's try one more time," my dad directed.

Harry crouched down and let out another high-pitched squeak. My dad frowned, showing his disappointment.

I stepped forward, bent down, and roared. I wanted to show him how it was done. However, I could see the fear in his eyes at my ferociousness.

My dad also noticed his anxiousness and ended the roughhousing. "That's enough for one day," he said, turning to my mother and leaning into her lovingly.

I caught my breath when he whispered, "I'm worried about him..."

"Oh, Abioye..." my mother sighed. Harry needs to be himself. You need to understand that everyone is different, and he shouldn't feel pressured to conform to your expectations. Pushing him to be tougher when it doesn't come naturally will affect his self-esteem."

My dad nodded in understanding.

"Give him the support to grow at his own pace." My mother looked at Harry with unconditional love.

My dad kissed her, acknowledging her saddened heart. Then, his gaze shifted toward me, a mix of guilt and resolve etched on his features. His voice, usually robust and confident, wavered slightly as he addressed me.

"Look after your brother today," he urged, his concern for Harry evident in his tone.

His eyes mirrored the guilt within him—the regret at having pushed Harry too hard, the understanding of his mistake, and the hope that I could provide the support he had failed to give.

I nodded in understanding.

"It's time for the nursery."

"Okay, Dad."

"Be gentle with Axle. He's in pain."

I nodded as a frown crossed my face, thinking about how the humans had hurt him. As my dad exited the cage, I turned and stared at my brother with mixed emotions. I didn't understand everything my mother had said to my father. I knew I wasn't supposed to be listening, but how could I not? Harry was always timid, and his demeanor contrasted with the other boy animals in the circus. His shyness embarrassed me, and I wished he were tougher. I wanted him to be like everyone else.

"Jett, it's time to leave," Mom ordered.

"Yes," I replied, gesturing toward Harry.

We kissed her goodbye and left, thrilled to spend the day with our friends.

On our way to the nursery, we saw Morton devouring a hotdog. After he finished, he stood and let out a loud belch, rubbing his protruding stomach. Within seconds, tiredness overcame him. We watched as he hid beside the "funnel cake" stand and fell into a deep sleep.

Harry and I couldn't help but laugh, seeing his swollen belly pointing toward the sky, mouth gaping, snoring loudly.

Hearing a grunt, we turned and saw Ziya, the male gorilla, standing on his hind legs inside his cage. He was snorting loudly at the ringmaster. As we passed them, Ziya continued to stare down Philip Andrews. The ringmaster became frightened and backed away from the cage.

"Calm down, Ziya!" he yelled.

Without warning, Ziya charged at the ringmaster from within his cage, causing Philip Andrews to stumble backward, emitting a high-pitched scream of terror.

"You do that again, and I'll turn you into mincemeat!" the ringmaster threatened.

Ziya responded with a loud grunt and pounded his chest aggressively. I quickly pulled Harry along, knowing we needed to get going. The ringmaster disapproved of us moving freely and insisted we remain in our cages.

Philip pointed and grimaced at Ziya one last time before heading toward the dining tent. It was time for his breakfast. I pulled my brother forward again to avoid being spotted, and we darted toward the nursery.

23

MOLLY

I WOKE UP with a start, brimming with excitement for my first day with the trainer. Trying to avoid disturbing Sofia and Bobbi-Cat's slumber, I silently slipped out of bed and onto the floor. However, my attempts proved futile as Bobbi-Cat lifted her head and awakened from a deep sleep.

"I'll come with you," she whispered.

Feeling grateful for the company, I smiled and nodded in agreement.

Gently pushing the door open, we slipped out unnoticed and went outside. As the circus animals stirred, the performers went to the dining tent. The aroma of breakfast wafted toward us, causing my stomach to grow hungry.

The dogs had already gathered and were eagerly waiting for their food. As we approached, Bobbi-Cat darted toward the side of the tent, spotting the ringmaster eating. I promised to save some food since she couldn't eat with us. She nodded and scampered into the shadows, knowing we would meet at the big top tent.

Once inside, I spotted Marceau with a warm smile on his face. He greeted me with a peck on the cheek and asked if I had slept well. I shook my head and told him that Chief's passing had kept me awake. He nodded sympathetically, adding that he hadn't slept either.

We sat down with the other dogs and waited for our bowls of kibble. I noticed the large poodle sitting to my right. However, he turned away as our gazes met, still angry that I was not showing any interest in him. I shook my head and rolled my eyes, thinking he was ridiculous.

I ate little, not wanting to be too full.

Marceau helped me sneak some food into my uniform pocket for Bobbi-Cat. Suddenly, I caught movement out of the corner of my eye and turned to see her scaling the wooden pole supporting the tent. I gasped, unsure of what she was doing.

I watched her walk along the ceiling beam and stop above the ringmaster. From there, she looked down and grimaced, her tail twitching with agitation.

As I watched, a mouse, not quite the size of Morton, scurried up behind her and began conversing. When Bobbi-Cat started giggling, I knew they were up to something.

The mouse leaped from the beam, landing on the table with a loud thud in front of the ringmaster.

Philip Andrews' face froze in shock when the mouse stood on its hind legs, put its paws on its ears, and stuck out its tongue.

The ringmaster released a high-pitched scream and fell backward in his chair, creating a commotion. As he composed himself, the mouse bit into his link sausage and scurried away. Everyone in the tent laughed, much to the ringmaster's dismay.

Among the laughter, Rosie's was the most distinct and boisterous. Turning, I saw her seated next to the "World's Tallest Man." Their shoulders brushed lightly, and there was an unmistakable spark of interest between them.

Turning back to the ringmaster, he stood up, dusted off his uniform, and glared angrily at everyone.

As Bobbi-Cat dashed undetected along the beam, the ringmaster flung his napkin onto the table, exasperated, and stomped out of the tent. The circus performers became quiet, observing his departure, satisfied that he received his well-deserved comeuppance.

After saying goodbye to Marceau, I headed to the big top tent. Upon arrival, I saw Bobbi-Cat waiting for me at the entrance. I gave her breakfast, and we laughed about her antics. She explained she would watch but stay out of sight. I nodded and entered the tent.

◆◆◆

The trainer politely introduced himself and wished me a good morning. Wasting no time, we began practicing my new circus act. He mentioned that if I could master it quickly, I would perform in today's matinee.

Excitement grew inside me as the trainer started me off by running, executing three forward flips and three backflips, and finishing by jumping through three hoops. Throughout the session, he was delighted with my energy and eagerness to learn. After mastering all the floor aerobics, he motioned toward a platform.

Upon setting foot on the wooden plank, it started ascending. Once it halted, I discovered I was 125 feet in the air. The high altitude messed with my vision. After inhaling deeply and soothing my anxiety, I stabilized myself and anticipated my next instruction.

The trainer signaled for me to jump.

I closed my eyes, bracing myself for the death-defying act. The stakes were sky-high, and failure wasn't an option. It all came down to this pivotal moment. I had to prove my worth or return to the dreary confines of the animal shelter. With a deep breath, I opened my eyes and leaped forward.

The world turned into a blur as I launched myself into the stunt. The air whipped past my fur, its fingers tugging at me, trying to pull me off course. But I was resolute and focused on the task at hand.

The trainer gasped as I twisted mid-air, my body contorting into impossible shapes as I executed a complex series of flips and spins. The world around me became a dizzying whirl of colors and sounds, but I kept my eyes fixed on my goal.

The cheer of my trainer faded into a distant hum, drowned out by the rush of adrenaline pumping through my veins. Then, just as quickly as it had begun, it was over. With one final, triumphant flip, I landed on the safety net. Relief washed over me like a tidal wave, quickly replaced by a surge of pride that swelled in my chest. I looked up at my trainer, who clapped enthusiastically with a wide smile.

I came to understand the genuine essence of courage. It wasn't about not feeling fear but conquering it. When Bobbi-Cat raced toward me, her eyes brimming with happiness, I experienced immense joy. Since joining the circus, my existence has shifted from roaming the streets to experiencing a sense of unity and belonging.

I treasured our newfound connection as I returned to Sofia's trailer with Bobbi-Cat. Shortly after arriving, Marceau and Cody joined us, and we settled for a nap together. At that moment, my heart overflowed with contentment. I realized that this was now my family, and a feeling of appreciation filled me.

24

CODY

WHILE RESTING in Sofia's bed before the matinee, we huddled together when a noise suddenly shattered the tranquil atmosphere. Roused from my slumber by the eerie creaking of the door, I slowly lifted my head and saw a strange, ominous, tall figure entering the trailer. My heart raced as I noticed the mysterious object he was carrying—a catchpole. With a surge of adrenaline, I leaped out of bed and shouted for everyone to wake up.

The dogcatcher burst into the trailer—his face contorted into an expression of sheer malevolence. His eyes burned with a cold, ruthless gleam, clearly irritated that I had awakened everyone. Behind him, Philip Andrews rushed in, equally upset.

"The Tabby!" he shouted, pointing at Bobbi-Cat.

In a panic, I turned and hollered for her to run. Despite her efforts, the dogcatcher's pole snatched her up as she darted through the trailer. She hissed and clawed at the animal control officer to free herself, but the cold, unyielding metal of the catchpole showed no mercy. She was now his captive.

The dogcatcher's face twisted into a vile sneer, relishing his capture with a dark, unsettling delight. His eyes, cold and devoid of empathy, seemed to take pleasure in the fear and chaos he wrought. His presence loomed over us, a tangible shadow of dread.

The horrifying scene unfolded in mere seconds. We watched in shock as they exited the trailer and wondered what had happened. Molly, overwhelmed with emotion, started sobbing uncontrollably, pleading for Bobbi-Cat's release.

Marceau attempted to comfort her, but his emotions betrayed him. He couldn't contain the fear and anger bubbling within him. Without a second thought, he bolted toward the retreating figures.

"Come back!" Molly's terrified scream echoed through the air, laced with the dread that they might take him too.

As Marceau returned, I could no longer stand idle. My heart pounded like a drum as I sprinted through the open door, my paws barely touching the ground.

I caught up with them just as the menacing figure of the dogcatcher shoved Bobbi-Cat into a metal cage perched atop a flatbed truck. The harsh clang of the cage door echoed ominously.

Bobbi-Cat let out a heart-wrenching meow. Her eyes were wide with fear, fully aware of her grim destination—the animal shelter. The sound resonated deep within me, stirring a primal urge to protect and rescue.

Suddenly, like a guardian angel, Sofia Bartolini materialized, her eyes wide with desperation as she pleaded with the animal control officer to release her. However, the ringmaster stepped in, his voice booming, declaring she was on report for defying his orders. Crushed and distraught, Sofia retreated, wiping away tears.

"Please don't do this..." Sofia begged.

As the dogcatcher turned his attention to Philip Andrews, I seized the opportunity and made a bold, impulsive decision. With my heart pounding, I dashed forward and leaped onto the back of the truck.

Bobbi-Cat looked up at me, her eyes wide with fear. I quickly hushed her. She retreated into the corner of the cage as I fumbled with the latch, flipping it open.

"Follow me!" I whispered urgently.

Without hesitation, Bobbie-Cat sprang from the cage, and together, we jumped off the truck, narrowly avoiding detection by the ringmaster and the dogcatcher. From the corner of my eye, I caught Sofia's gaze. Seeing us escape, her eyes lit up with relief, and she struggled to suppress a triumphant giggle.

"Let's head toward Rosie's trailer," I shouted, my voice tense with urgency. We sprinted away from the nightmarish scene, and within minutes, we found ourselves inside our destination.

Rosie noticed us as we entered, her eyes full of concern, wondering about our unexpected appearance.

Desperate to convey what had happened, I began meowing incessantly. Even though she couldn't understand my words, Bobbie-Cat's look suggested imminent danger.

I couldn't stop meowing until Rosie assured me, she'd protect Bobbie-Cat.

Feeling a wave of relief wash over me, I brushed against her with a gentle nudge, my fur softly grazing her leg in a gesture of heartfelt thanks.

Bobbie-Cat approached me, her eyes glowing like two emerald moons, reflecting a deep gratitude that words could never express. She looked at me—her gaze soft and warm as she thanked me for coming to her rescue.

But I saw more than gratitude in her eyes. It was love—a deep, unspoken connection that resonated between us. It warmed my heart, making my paws tingle with an emotion I had never felt before—an emotion so strong it threatened to consume me.

I moved closer and gently pressed my nose to hers. Her scent, sweet and familiar, overwhelmed my senses.

"As much as I want you to watch my performance," I explained, barely above a whisper, "I need you to stay here. It's unsafe!" The words were hard to say, but I knew they were necessary. I cared too much about her to put her in any danger. I wanted her to be safe, even if we had to be apart for a while.

"Oh..." she said, disappointment in her voice.

It was clear my words saddened her. She wanted to be near me.

"I can't hide for the rest of my life."

"Understand!" I exclaimed. "After I return, we'll talk and plan our future. If we must, we'll leave the circus..."

Bobbie-Cat nodded. Tears filled her eyes.

With the matinee performance still a few hours away, we huddled on Rosie's bed. I tenderly groomed her fur and whispered sweet words of love into her ear.

Bobbie-Cat purred contentedly.

However, thoughts of the ringmaster and his actions filled me with rage. How dare he call the animal shelter on her? It made little sense. As far as he knew, she was doing her job of keeping the rodent population at bay.

Suddenly, I realized. Felicia must have said something to him. Everything abruptly made sense.

I kept this revelation to myself and stayed by her until it was time for my performance. As I prepared to leave, I kissed her forehead, saying I'd return shortly.

She nodded in understanding.

Before departing, I meowed, expressing my gratitude to Rosie.

"You're welcome!" she replied warmly.

My heart ached for the human. She was the kindest, most compassionate person, yet she had to endure the humiliating role of a "Freak Show" act. The gasps and horrified stares from the paying audience were a cruel reminder of her fate. It pained her deeply, just as it did her fellow sideshow friends. It was unjust, but they had no choice—they needed to make a living.

25

ELSA

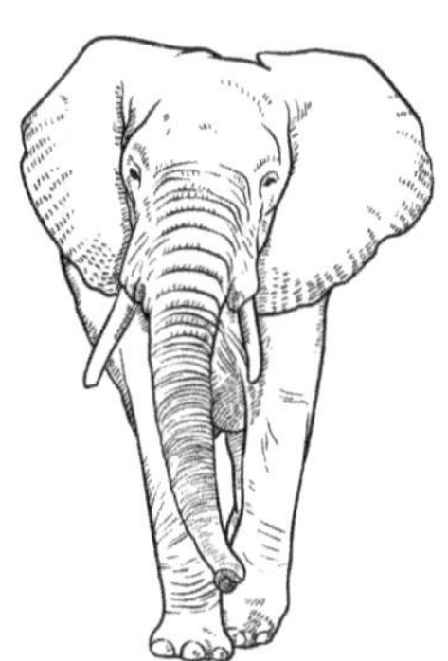

A S I SLOWLY WOKE from our afternoon nap, the heart-wrenching sound of Luca's cries filled my ears. I turned toward him, taking in the sight of his body trembling uncontrollably. His breaths were coming in quick gasps, a clear sign he was in the throes of a distressing nightmare.

"Mommy... wh-where are you?" he stuttered out, his voice filled with fear and confusion as he remained trapped within the confines of his dream world.

I gently called "Luca?" to rouse him from his troubled slumber. As I shifted my position to sit up more comfortably, my foot unintentionally landed on Jett's front paw. He responded instantly with a piercing yelp of pain.

"Get off me!" he roared in response, his voice filled with surprise and hurt.

Startled by his outcry, I hastily retracted my foot and asked with genuine concern, "Are you all right?"

Jett gingerly lifted his paw, his expression twisted with pain. The discomfort seemed to intensify as he flexed it. Ablaze with resentment, his eyes pierced me with an accusatory stare that penetrated my soul.

"You broke my paw," Jett declared.

"Oh, no…"

He emphatically stated that this injury would leave him permanently disabled, preventing him from walking or ever playing again. His words hung in the air with an ominous finality, as if my inadvertent action had sealed his unfortunate fate.

Overwhelmed with guilt, I couldn't help but gasp. "I didn't mean to hurt you," I choked out through a sudden onslaught of tears, heartbroken that I had caused him pain.

Jett leaned in close, his brow furrowed in a display of bitterness.

"You weigh too much!" he snapped sharply, his words cutting through the silence.

Feeling the sting of his harsh words, I hung my head low—the pain penetrating deep within my heart. At this moment, Mia stepped forward, openly chastising Jett for his spiteful remark.

"You're acting like a baby! Your paw's not broken," she retorted defiantly, giving him a pointed look that dared him to argue further.

Her words seemed to stoke the fire in him, and he confronted her in an intimidating manner. As I gasped in surprise again, Harry stepped forward to defend Mia. He boldly told his brother to leave her alone, which took Jett aback and caused his demeanor to turn for the worse.

"What did you just say?" he growled ominously.

The confrontation left Harry speechless and visibly frightened. As he stepped back in shock, tears welled up in his eyes. Seeing his distress, Mia raised her voice, shouting at Jett to behave himself.

Axle, observing the conflict quietly, slowly stood up and intervened. He made a calming gesture, urging us to stop fighting. I sighed heavily, noting the visible pain reflected in his stance.

"There's no need to be unkind," Axle said sternly. "You must learn to be compassionate with each other."

We all took Axle's words to heart, letting them resonate deeply within us. As Mia and I walked away, she tried to comfort me.

"That was so cruel," I mumbled, feeling the weight of Jett's words.

"You didn't deserve that," Mia consoled, leaning her long neck against me.

I felt comforted by her reassurance.

Reflecting on this experience, I realized that no one should have to endure verbal abuse because of their weight. Jett's hurtful words had a significant impact on my self-esteem.

Despite feeling upset with Jett, my concern for his well-being was undeniable. My heart ached as I watched him wander into the pen with his head lowered. "Oh, Jett..." I cried, knowing he felt rejected by us. The urge to break away and comfort him was strong, but Mia pulled me forward, shaking her head.

"He must deal with the consequences of his actions."

"He doesn't know any better..."

"Let him be..."

"Okay..." I muttered.

"Let's go play with Luca..."

As we began walking, my heart broke at the sight of Axle comforting Luca. Looking closely at Axle, I could see the pain and sadness etched on his face. It was heart-wrenching to witness. The loss of Chief had profoundly affected him.

From the beginning, I sensed Axle was different. I brought it up to my mother when I couldn't figure it out. She explained that, just like some humans, some animals loved others of the same sex. She said love wasn't confined by gender, and what truly mattered was the connection between two souls. I immediately understood her words. Axle's attraction to other male dogs didn't bother me—it made me love him even more.

Luca looked up to see us.

I reached out my trunk and teased him. He smiled, stood, and playfully nibbled at me. It was all good fun.

Axle stepped back, grateful that we had come to help. As he watched, he lay down—his stillness was heartbreaking.

26

FELICIA

LYING IN MY ENCLOSURE, I lifted my head, only to be met with a wave of dizziness. I couldn't comprehend why I felt so terrible. When the trainer opened the cage this morning, I remained inside. I meowed, expressing my fatigue, but he paid no attention. I understood I had a reputation for being a diva, making me the least favored feline.

Struggling to stand, my stomach roiled, and I ended up vomiting. What was happening? The matinee performance was fast approaching. I hadn't eaten, my balance was off, and I felt bloated. Was I gaining weight?

I contemplated the scenario, remembering that I adhered to a strict diet to maintain my lean figure and was always cautious about indulging in post-meal treats.

Distracted, I scratched my belly and flinched from a sudden, sharp pain that coursed through me. Glancing down, I noticed my teats had become swollen. Gasping, I took a deep breath and tried to piece together what might be happening.

"Oh, no," I murmured, a whisper barely escaping my lips. The realization was slow, creeping up on me like the first light of dawn after a long night. My mind wandered, adrift in a sea of memories from a month ago.

We had been touring, our days filled with performances and our nights with restlessness. The city we were visiting was one of many lost amidst a whirlwind journey that had taken us through many states. Each town was a blur, a melting pot of faces and places that merged into one. Yet, one place—an alleyway in a forgotten corner of one of those cities—remained etched in my memory.

It was there, hidden away from the circus's hustle and bustle, that I met Tom. He was a captivating alley cat, charm as alluring as the moonlight that bathed the alleyway. His approach was bold, almost audacious, but it held an intrigue that was impossible to resist. His eyes sparkled with mischief and adventure, drawing me into his world.

In the alleyway's seclusion, away from the prying eyes of the circus troupe, we found ourselves drawn to each other. His purrs were whispers in my ear, his touch a tantalizing caress against my fur. We danced under the moonlight, our bodies swaying to a rhythm as old as time. It was a passionate encounter, a union of two souls under the starry night. One thing led to another, and soon enough, our connection deepened into something more.

The trailer door creaked open, disrupting my thoughts. A veterinarian walked in—his face etched with concern. I hadn't shown up for my performance, and the ringmaster had sent him to check on me. The moment of truth was upon me—my secret was about to be unveiled. My heart pounded in my chest as I waited for the inevitable.

The silent walls of the trailer echoed with unspoken words, and I could only brace myself for what was to come.

27

BOBBI-CAT

A S I HID BENEATH the bleachers in the big top tent, the animated crowd eagerly awaited the matinee's start. Circus music blared through the loudspeakers, filling the air with its melody. Fresh popcorn and sizzling hotdogs wafted through the stands as children excitedly munched on their treats. The anticipation in the atmosphere was unmistakable, spreading like wildfire among the spectators.

Excitement coursed through me as I gazed at the three rings in the center of the enormous tent. In no time, these rings would come alive with captivating performances.

Taking a deep breath, I knew I shouldn't be here. The ringmaster was present, and if he caught sight of me, he would take me away for good. Once Rosie left the trailer, I made a break for the tent. I couldn't stay behind, even knowing Cody would be upset.

As the music abruptly ceased, a deep drum roll resonated through the tent, causing the chatter and excitement to taper off to a hush. All eyes were on the center ring, waiting for the performance to begin. The announcer's voice boomed through the speakers, welcoming everyone and heralding the beginning of an unforgettable experience. As the spotlight illuminated the stage, the ringmaster emerged, commanding the attention and respect of the audience. He took a gracious bow as the crowd broke into thunderous applause.

With bated breath, I rushed outside, awaiting the start of Molly's performance with the circus dogs. I couldn't help but feel a pang of nervousness for her. But as I approached, I spotted Marceau, who doted on her with tenderness and love, helping to calm her nerves. A wave of warmth flowed through me as I observed their perfect partnership and knew that they would be together forever.

The trainer snapped his fingers, and the dogs lined up two by a row with Marceau and Molly at the front. As the trainer blew his whistle, the dogs scampered into the tent. I ran after them, darting underneath the bleachers to avoid the audience and the ringmaster's eyes.

Sitting down, I watched the dogs enter the center ring, jumping onto raised platforms. The trainer acknowledged the audience with a bow and began the act. The spectators clapped as he pointed toward Molly, who was surprisingly the first to perform. I couldn't take my eyes off her as she jumped off her platform, performed three front flips, stopped, and immediately executed three backflips in a row with breathtaking agility.

As the audience cheered, the trainer lit a torch to build excitement, igniting three large hoops. The flames were high and menacing, and I held my breath as a drum roll began. The trainer motioned Molly forward, and she took off running. Still holding my breath, I watched her jump through the first, second, and last—third hoop without harm. I exhaled in relief as she sat down, waiting for her following command.

The audience fell in love with her. Molly was entirely in her element, performing again in front of an audience. The trainer blew his whistle and pointed toward the rising platform. Molly ran to it and sat down, lifting her right paw into the air. The audience gasped in amazement, knowing she was about to perform a death-defying act—high diving from 125 feet in the air.

I didn't know whether to close my eyes out of nervousness for her. The drum roll continued and finally stopped as the platform reached its height. The audience stared upward, excited at what they were about to witness. Molly looked so small, so far away. If it hadn't been for the spotlight, no one would have been able to see her. Everyone held their breath as Molly rose on her hind legs, ready to make a leap of faith.

As the drum roll began again, I held my breath, watching my friend leap off the platform and into the air. Astonishingly, she grabbed her hind legs and flipped in continuous circles as she descended toward the ground. Just before reaching the safety net, she released her legs, flawlessly executing a graceful triple flip that brought joy to everyone's eyes.

The drum roll suddenly stopped, and the cymbals clashed when she landed on the net, bouncing upwards. Standing upright, she jumped to the ground, raised her right paw, and beamed from ear to ear. The audience cheered and applauded, celebrating Molly's incredible performance.

My heart swelled with pride, watching Molly's breathtaking act. Tears fell as I couldn't help but admire her. I sat on my hind legs and clapped alongside the audience, yelling, "Bravo! Bravo!" as loudly as I could, hoping she could hear me over the crowd. Molly was unstoppable, and her determination and courage knew no bounds.

◆◆◆

The cats strolled into the center ring as the dogs exited the big top tent. My eyes fixed on Cody, the largest cat in the show. His magnificent coat was on display for everyone to admire. Suddenly, I realized Felicia wasn't in line and wondered what had happened. She would always attend a performance, so something must be wrong. Shaking the thoughts of Felicia from my mind, I watched as Cody and his substitute began the show.

The acrobatic performance unfolding before my eyes was nothing short of breathtaking. With his well-defined muscles rippling beneath his glossy fur, Cody executed each move gracefully and precisely, leaving me in awe. His strength, as he effortlessly hoisted his partner into the air, was a testament to his physical prowess.

Cody was larger than most cats—a fact that was easily noticeable even from a distance. The sight of him, so strong and confident, sent a wave of excitement coursing through me.

Reflecting on my past relationships, it became increasingly clear how different Cody was. He was unlike any cat I had ever known—his kindness and nurturing nature set him apart from the rest. His love for me was apparent in every glance, every touch, and every word.

As Cody sprinted across the floor, his movements were fluid and graceful, and I held my breath. His dramatic floor routine was a mesmerizing display of agility and strength. How he moved, leaped, and twisted in the air was a sight to behold.

Finally, with a flourish, he completed his act. A sense of pride swelled within me as he bowed to the applauding audience. There he was, the embodiment of feline perfection—Cody, the cat who had captured my heart.

I stood on my hind legs and shouted, "Bravo" once more, clapping as loudly as possible. But then I noticed the ringmaster looking in my direction. I quickly crouched down, realizing my mistake. The stomping of feet and the crowd's cheers caused the ringmaster to turn toward the audience and smile. He was in his element. His narcissism surfaced as he took credit for all the animals' hard work. It was all about him.

My mood shifted upon realizing this. The unsuspecting crowd did not know what the animals endured. Knowing how the ringmaster treated them and how hard they worked to master their act broke my heart. I realized I was fortunate—I had no job, and Sofia cared for me. A pang of guilt washed over me as I came to this realization.

Contemplating our future, I knew Cody and I couldn't stay here any longer. Recognizing how much Cody loved performing, guilt again swept through me. The thought of taking him away from his dream overwhelmed me. A tear welled in my eye as I realized I couldn't do that to him.

28

MOLLY

ALOUD, INTRUSIVE BURP abruptly halted the conversation between Marceau and me as we quenched our thirst at the watering trough. We glanced upward to find Frank and George, the Black Heron duo, perched above us. Frank, looking mortified, covered his beak and apologized for his distasteful belch.

"That cherry didn't sit well with my stomach!" he exclaimed, attempting to justify his rudeness.

George rolled his eyes and shook his head, clearly unimpressed by his friend's theatrical display. Despite ourselves, Marceau and I broke into laughter. However, our amusement was short-lived as vocal chanting erupted from the distance.

Marceau and I exchanged puzzled glances as the noise grew louder. Before long, a group of disgruntled circus performers aggressively marched toward the big tent, their voices merging into a loud chorus of "Strike! Strike! Strike!"

It was clear they were protesting their unjust wages and unfavorable working conditions. As the audience vacated the tent, the protest grew louder, tainting the air with disquiet.

Philip Andrews emerged from the tent with a visibly distressed expression, attempting to dissolve the gathering, realizing the harmful impact this demonstration would have on the circus's reputation.

"Strike! Strike! Strike!" the chant echoed relentlessly.

The ringmaster, known for his authoritative voice and commanding aura, seemed to falter under the collective scrutiny of the discontented performers. The boy, whose face bore an uncanny resemblance to a canine, suddenly broke the tense silence. His words, sharp and accusatory, cut through the atmosphere like daggers.

"Step down!"

Usually cheerful and bubbly, Rosie chimed in with a grim expression and voiced her complaint.

"You're starving us! Look at me. I'm losing weight!"

To pacify the crowd, the ringmaster raised his hands and explained their dire financial situation following the loss of Taya and Mischa. His voice wavered, reflecting the fear and uncertainty that gripped everyone.

Suddenly, Sofia Bartolini, the esteemed ring mistress, emerged. Her large, worried eyes swept over the crowd.

Unexpectedly, the "Bearded Lady," a woman of great size and bravery, moved to the front. She carried a sign that proclaimed, "We want Sofia as our ringmaster." The placard sparked cheers throughout the gathering.

The situation escalated dramatically when the ringmaster pulled out a pistol. The weapon's metallic glint under the midway lights sent ripples of terror through everyone. He raised the gun above his head, his face twisted in a grotesque display of jealousy and rage. Once a place of joy and laughter, the circus had abruptly transformed into a battleground with an uncertain outcome.

"We're bankrupt, people!" he shouted, his voice echoing ominously.

"He's got a gun!" Rosie screamed, bolting from the scene as the ringmaster fired a shot into the air.

The crowd dispersed, with the exiting spectators screaming and fleeing in every direction, creating utter chaos. Those who remained held their breath, uncertain of what would happen next.

Marceau and I stared at each other in disbelief.

The ringmaster lowered the gun, and shouted, "I'm in charge here. Stop this foolishness and get back to work. This is not a request—it's an order!"

Some of the protesters, intimidated by his threats, left, while most stayed and resumed chanting. I could see the fear in the ringmaster's eyes as he realized he was losing control of the situation.

Suddenly, my thoughts shifted to the little ones. "The babies!" I shouted, and without another word, Marceau and I bolted toward the nursery. We knew the kids would be distressed, and chaos would ensue. As we navigated through the crowd, people were stumbling and falling over one another, transforming the previously serene scene into a dangerous battlefield.

Amid this chaos, a little human girl fell to the pavement. I paused momentarily to check on her, but her mother scooped her up and whisked her away. As we continued our desperate dash, Marceau yelped in pain when someone stepped on him. He gestured for me to continue, and I resumed running, hoping he'd catch up.

Upon reaching safety, I turned around anxiously, scanning for any sign of Marceau. A relieved smile spread across my face when I spotted him running toward me.

"Are you all right?" he asked, concerned.

I responded with a simple nod—my mind preoccupied with apprehension.

Marceau's eyes widened in understanding, and without wasting another moment, we continued toward the nursery. As we neared the pen, the distant cries of the babies reached my ears, sending shivers down my spine. When they came into view, my heart sank at the sight of their terrified faces. The once peaceful circus that I called home was now a chaotic mess.

29

MORTON

A SHARP AND STARTLING gunshot jolted me from my slumber, and fear gripped me, momentarily paralyzing me. As my eyes adjusted, I realized I had dozed off after indulging in a hotdog. Embarrassment washed over me, and I glanced around, hoping no one had seen me.

The gravity of my selfishness sank in. Taya and Mischa's lives were in danger, and I had fallen asleep. Panic surged within me when I realized I'd been out for hours.

Wiping the sweat off my forehead, I ran toward the nursery. I maneuvered through the crowd, ensuring my safety amidst the chaos.

As I reached the pen, I spotted Axle gathering everyone together for protection. Without hesitation, I rushed toward him, screaming at the top of my lungs, "TAYA AND MISCHA ARE AT BIRD ISLAND IN AUDUBON PARK!"

Startled by a second gunshot, I dove under his belly, but my protruding stomach caused me to fall to the ground. Blushing from embarrassment, I picked myself up on all fours and crawled underneath him.

Peering out, I saw fear etched on the babies' faces. It was clear they were just as terrified as I was.

Axle looked down, questioning my cowardice. "You should be ashamed of yourself," he declared, his words echoing in my ears.

I suddenly gasped as the weight of my behavior crashed down on me. I was an adult mouse, and it was clear that I needed to lend a helping hand. Slowly and carefully, I extricated myself from beneath him. As I raised my head, I was met with several innocent stares.

Embarrassed, I offered the babies a sheepish smile and a small wave. To my surprise, they didn't seem to perceive my cowardice. However, this realization didn't make me feel any better—instead, it heightened my guilt. These young, vulnerable kids needed protection, and I, a mature mouse, acted selfishly. All I had thought about was myself.

Immense guilt fell upon me. I had a specific purpose—to alert Axle about Taya and Mischa's location. But I had failed miserably in my task. Taking a deep breath, I tried to shake off the heavy blanket of remorse that was threatening to suffocate me.

"What can I do to help?" I asked, turning my gaze toward Axle.

"Help me gather them together," he requested, his voice weary.

I responded with a firm nod, reaching out my paws to the little ones. It took a few moments, but eventually, everyone calmed down. With Axle leading the way, we herded them toward the safety of the shed.

30

AXLE

WITH MORTON'S HELP, we rounded up the babies and ushered them to the shed for protection. As I pushed the door open and looked back, the unmistakable fear on everyone's faces was clear. "Get in the shed," I commanded.

Mia exclaimed, "I'm scared!"

Turning to Morton with a firm look, I said, "Everything will be fine. Morton will stay and protect you."

"Are you leaving, Axle?" Jett asked.

"I'm going to save Taya and Mischa."

"We'll come with you," Luca stammered.

"Everyone's staying here!"

As sadness filled the youngster's faces, Elsa murmured, "You need help."

Placing a reassuring paw on her foot, I gently replied, "I'll be fine. I need you to stay here where it's safe."

"But Axle..." Elsa moaned.

"It's too dangerous."

At that moment, Marceau and Molly came barging into the nursery.

"You're not going alone," Marceau exclaimed, having overheard the conversation.

Molly chimed in, "We're coming with you!"

The little ones gasped at being left behind.

As I turned toward them, I noticed mischief brewing in their minds. However, understanding their eagerness for adventure, I ignored them and pointed inside the shed.

They hesitated initially but soon followed my directions. Once inside, they stopped, anxiously waiting for Morton. Suddenly, another shot echoed, causing Morton to panic. He screamed, threw his paws over his head, and dashed in the opposite direction.

"Oh, Morton..." I sighed.

"We'll be fine..." Elsa murmured, shutting the door behind them.

With the babies now secured, I gave Marceau and Molly a confirming nod, indicating my readiness to depart.

We left the babies safely in the pen and carefully navigated through the protesters, silently passing by as their chants filled the air. Suddenly, the contortionist stepped out and pointed aggressively at the ringmaster with an expression of intense hostility, which brought us to a standstill.

"You're mistreating the animals!" he thundered.

In a bid for solidarity, the ringmaster gestured for Sofia to stand beside him. However, fueled by indignation, she rebuffed him with a succinct yet impactful declaration.

"I quit!"

Her announcement dramatically transformed the situation. The demonstrators cheered as she crossed the picket line to stand among them.

"Keep moving!" I whispered under my breath, aware of the urgency to hasten our departure. A lengthy voyage lay before us.

31

BOBBI-CAT

A S I MEANDERED toward the exit of the circus grounds, my thoughts lingered on Cody. Leaving him was hard, but deep down, I understood it was for the best—his passion for performing was undeniable, and without it, he would surely wither. I stopped near the nursery and noticed Elsa peering out from the shed door.

When she emerged, she motioned for the occupants to follow. I couldn't resist my curiosity and found a hidden spot to uncover the unfolding secret.

As the babies emerged from the shed, Elsa began to whisper. I held my breath, trying to catch every word.

"I have concerns," she murmured, glancing nervously around. "Axle won't make the journey."

"What do you mean?" Luca asked.

"We need to follow them!" she insisted, her eyes bright with determination.

"Are you crazy?" Harry exclaimed, his eyes bulging with terror. "There's a swamp in Audubon Park! What about the alligators?"

Jett stepped forward, his eyes rolling in a blatant display of exasperation. "Stop acting like a baby," he sneered.

"Leave me alone!" Harry shot back.

Jett nudged his brother's shoulder.

"I'm going to tell Dad!" Harry retorted, his voice trembling with escalating fear.

Jett contorted his face into a feigned expression and raised his paws in a fluttering motion to ridicule his brother's nervousness.

"I'm going to tell Dad!"

"Jett, stop it!" Elsa shouted, her voice ringing out sharply against his cruel behavior.

Harry's face flushed a deep crimson, his eyes flashing with humiliation. His paws balled tightly as he battled to suppress the welling tears.

"You're nothing but a bully!" Elsa exclaimed.

Jett gasped, his bravado faltering under the unexpected weight of the accusation. Mia advanced on him, her face inches from his.

"You hurt Elsa's feelings this morning and haven't even apologized. Harry idolizes you. Why are you so mean to him?"

I turned to Jett. His eyes welled up, brimming with a shame he'd never fully acknowledged until now.

"We should leave," murmured Elsa. Turning to Jett, she added, "If you can't behave, stay here!"

I gasped in surprise.

"What about our parents?" Harry asked.

Elsa furrowed her brow in deep thought. "That's a good point... However, we'll lose them if we don't leave now."

"My mom's going to be upset," Harry sobbed, his eyes gleaming with unshed tears.

"Everything will be fine," Jett assured him.

"This isn't a good idea," Harry continued, hastily wiping his eyes with the back of his paw.

Breaking his silence, Luca stepped forward and spoke authoritatively. "I... I agree with Elsa... We should get going."

"Oh, my..." I murmured, the gravity of their resolution sinking in. With a swift movement, I sprang to my feet and darted after them.

In what felt like no time, they exited the circus grounds and encountered a directional road sign that said "Audubon Park—Bird Island & Zoo." It immediately grabbed everyone's attention.

While they were trying to figure out the sign's meaning, I noticed Morton on the sidewalk, with his nose buried in a pile of discarded popcorn. When he saw the babies, he lowered his head, trying to look inconspicuous.

When he looked up, he peered through his paws as if attempting to evade their notice. Observing Morton, he returned to his popcorn, trying to ignore them. However, after a few seconds, he gasped.

"Gosh, darn it!" he yelled, raising his paws in resignation.

I crouched behind a fire hydrant as everyone noticed him striding toward them with determination, his narrowed eyes showing frustration.

"Where do you think you're going?" he demanded, his voice a mix of authority and exasperation.

"Axle needs our help," Jett replied.

Morton ignored Jett's comment and glared at the group. "You've lost your minds!"

"No, we haven't!" Elsa murmured.

"You don't even know where you're going," Morton criticized, escalating frustration.

"We're going to Bird Island in Audubon Park," Mia responded confidently, her eyes sparkling excitedly.

Emphasizing his frustration, Morton raised his paws in a dramatic display. "Do you know where that is?" he questioned, his voice rising an octave.

All the babies nodded vigorously, pointing in different directions, their enthusiasm undeterred by Morton's skepticism.

Morton bent forward, holding his chest, and made overly dramatic wheezing noises. "It's two miles away!" he breathed.

Alarmed, Elsa stepped forward, her eyes wide with concern. "Are you okay?"

"My heart! This is too much!" Morton exclaimed, pointing toward Bird Island. "IT'S THAT WAY!"

"Oh…" Everyone gasped.

Taking a deep breath, Morton assessed the situation. The babies were determined to proceed, regardless of his objections. With this realization setting in, he glared at everyone.

"You need to follow me," he declared, his voice firm and unyielding. "I'm in charge here. We're heading home immediately if anyone steps out of line or misbehaves."

His tone was firm, leaving no room for argument. The playful chatter ceased, replaced by a collective nod of agreement.

As Morton led the way, I followed and stayed in the background. I realized this adventure would be a valuable learning experience for everyone. With Morton in charge, I decided to intervene only if necessary.

The fresh air and the sweet scent of blooming flowers welcomed me as I entered Audubon Park. It was a picture-perfect evening that filled my heart with joy. As I strolled along the winding path, a delightful sight caught my eye—the babies frolicking in the open space. They were having a grand time, running around and chasing each other in their playful abandon. I couldn't help but smile as I watched them, admiring their boundless energy and infectious playfulness.

After their lively play session, they ventured further into the park under Morton's watchful guidance. The growing darkness cloaked the path ahead, but it wasn't a cause for concern because lightning bugs illuminated the way. These small, glowing insects were a sight to behold. Their presence created a tranquil atmosphere, transforming our walk into a mesmerizing experience.

As we continued our journey, we came across a majestic oak tree, its grandeur standing against the night sky. A single lightning bug glowed gently on the commemoration plaque at its base.

Elsa leaned in and read the inscription.

"The locals refer to this as the 'Tree of Life.' They believe its age ranges between one hundred and five hundred years," she explained, her words resonating with a sense of awe.

Mia's eyes widened in disbelief, reflecting the light from the glowing bug. "That's as old as Axle," she exclaimed, her voice filled with wonder.

A giggle erupted from Jett, breaking the serene silence that had settled around us. "He's not that old," he retorted, his laughter echoing softly through the park, adding a touch of light-heartedness to our excursion.

As the little ones continued to joke and tease each other about Axle's age, they grew more comfortable in the darkness.

The "Tree of Life" was an imposing sight, its massive trunk gnarled with age. The bark was rough and thick. Its roots dug deep into the earth, providing a solid foundation.

Elsa reached upward with her trunk and grabbed the moss hanging from its branches. I watched as she opened her mouth to taste it, only to spit it out seconds later.

"Yuck!" she shouted, wiping her mouth continually to get the unpleasant taste out.

The moss landed on Morton, causing him to jump up and down in frustration.

"Elsa? Really?"

As everyone laughed, they suddenly turned, hearing a roar in the background. They became quiet and gathered, frightened by the sound.

It was a lion's roar.

The roar was deep, a guttural growl resonating with such intensity that it seemed to shake the ground beneath them. The sound was primal and commanding, a clear assertion of dominance that echoed through the air, causing their hearts to pound in their chests. I held my breath, waiting to see what happened next.

"What's that?" Mia asked.

"The New Orleans Zoo," Morton explained.

"The Ne-New Orleans Zoo?" Luca shouted—his eyes wide.

Morton confirmed, nodding his head.

"My mother's in there!" Luca exclaimed, and without hesitation, he darted off toward the zoo.

"Oh, my God!" I muttered under my breath, poised to give chase. But to my relief, the babies were quick to react. They called out for him to stop, their voices filled with concern for his safety. Like a pack, they chased after him. I let out a sigh of relief, grateful for their swift intervention.

"Luca..." Jett shouted.

Luca stopped and turned around, glancing at his friends. As the babies caught up, Jett stepped forward. His voice was soft and filled with compassion.

"It's too dangerous!"

"My mother's in there!" he cried, turning back toward the zoo. "I-I want my mother."

Everyone glanced at each other, feeling heartbroken. As tears fell from Luca's eyes, Jett consoled him.

"You're not alone. You have me," came his reassuring voice.

"Oh, Jett! You do have feelings," Mia exclaimed, stepping forward excitedly, hearing his endearing words.

"We're your family now," Harry declared with conviction.

"I know she's worried about me," Luca cried, sitting down while wiping the tears away with his hooves.

A deep sigh escaped from Morton as his heart filled with sadness. "I know you're hurting, but it's not safe. We can't go in without Axle."

"But..." Luca protested.

"I'm not big enough to protect you," Morton continued, a tear escaping his eye.

Luca sniffled.

"Do you understand?" Morton asked gently.

Nodding his head, Luca continued wiping his eyes. "I miss her so much."

At this, all the babies came together, offering support in Luca's time of need. Watching this scene unfold, I couldn't help but smile—my heart brimming with emotion from witnessing their profound love for him.

32

SOFIA

A HEAVY ACHE SETTLED in my heart for the parents of these little ones. I stood amidst them in the nursery, desperately trying to assuage their fears and concerns. Even though I was not a parent, I could comprehend the depths of their apprehension.

"Axle's not here. The babies must be with him," I explained. "He'll ensure their safety."

As I met each parent's gaze, I realized my words had done little to ease their worries. A profound sigh escaped me. Despite uncertainty about how to proceed, I knew we needed to stay together and support one another.

The protesters assembled around us, placing their placards on the ground. They, too, were aware of the gravity of the situation.

The boy with dog-like features announced his intention to build a bonfire. The other performers unanimously approved his suggestion. They resolved to stay and offer their support.

Everyone dispersed, scavenging for wood scraps. I remained with Mable, Abioye, Eshe, and Mia's parents.

The performers gradually trickled back—arms laden with an assortment of wooden debris that would fuel our fire.

The fire crackled and danced within no time, throwing stark shadows on our faces as we stood around it in silent solidarity. Our hearts echoed a singular prayer, pleading for the little one's safe return.

"Sofia?"

The deep, resonant voice broke through my thoughts. I turned to find the "Strongman" regarding me with a look of concern that softened his rugged features. He stood there, shirtless, under the glow of the firelight, revealing a physique that was nothing short of awe-inspiring.

As I took in the sight of him, my emotions unexpectedly surged to the surface. Tears welled up, spilling over and streaking down my cheeks. The gravity of the situation had finally caught up with me, and my control slipped, allowing raw vulnerability to seep through.

My soft sniffles broke the silence, drawing his concern. Seeing my tears, he stepped forward, his expression a mix of empathy.

He wrapped his powerful arms around me, pulling me into the warm embrace of his muscular chest. An unexpected sense of safety washed over me as I nestled into him. His scent—a comforting blend of sweat, smoke from the bonfire, and a subtle hint of something uniquely his—enveloped me, further deepening the feeling of security.

I wasn't alone anymore. I had him—this robust and caring man—by my side. My turmoil subsided, replaced by a growing sense of calm and resilience.

33

CODY

AFTER THE PERFORMANCE, I returned to Rosie's trailer, excited to see Bobbi-Cat. The moment I stepped inside, her absence was apparent, creating a void that filled the small space with silence. When Rosie returned, visibly shaken from the chaos outside, I meowed with urgency and despair, trying desperately to communicate Bobbi-Cat's disappearance. She enveloped me in a tight hug. Despite her comforting words, tears breached my eyes—revealing the depth of my vulnerability.

Moving to the rocking chair, she cradled me in her lap.

Eventually, the sharp scent of smoke pulled us outside to gather around the bonfire. Even in Rosie's secure embrace, the warmth of the fire couldn't melt the chill of realization settling over me—Bobbi-Cat wasn't the only one missing—Axle, Molly, Marceau, and the babies were gone too. The urge to search for Bobbi-Cat clawed at me, but Rosie's gentle hold kept me anchored as she whispered, her voice cracking with sorrow.

"She could be anywhere."

The weight of those words crushed me further. Resigned, I understood the painful truth. It was wiser to stay put and hold on to the hope of Bobbi-Cat's return, even as my heart ached with worry.

As the gentle warmth of the fire soothed all of us, a buzz of conversation caught my attention from behind. Curious, I turned to see the circus felines gathered in a lively group. Their chatter grew loud as they gossiped about Felicia, full of wild gestures and dramatic gasps. They avidly proclaimed that she was pregnant, attributing to her absence from today's matinee.

Their words, tinged with scandalous delight, painted vivid, absurd scenarios. One suggested she'd been moonlighting in a cathouse, while another speculated about a secret admirer from a rival circus. This kind of news would generally spark a mischievous smirk on my face, but the gnawing concern for Bobbi-Cat's whereabouts overshadowed any amusement.

I turned my back on their banter, finding their obnoxious speculations wrong. At that moment, my thoughts were solely with Bobbi-Cat.

Seeking solace in Rosie's arms, I meowed softly. She gazed down at me, her eyes twinkling with understanding. Her hand reached out, strokes soothing and deliberate, as she began petting me. I welcomed the comforting rhythm of her touch, letting my eyes close to still my racing heart.

34

BILLY-JOE

A S I SAT AROUND the campfire, Taya's deafening roars resonated in the background, draining the joy from my soul. Somewhat drunk, a wave of depression washed over me. Guilt gnawed at my conscience for unknowingly contributing to her abduction.

Deep in thought, I realized Sam had duped me into participating in this scheme. He was drunk on whiskey, seemingly oblivious to the gravity of his actions. When Taya roared again, I felt a pressing urge to ask what was wrong with her to gauge his reaction.

In response, Sam dismissively told me to stop fretting, infuriating me even further. Despite my intelligence, I was tired of him always being in charge and dictating my every move. "Why didn't you inform me you were in contact with a furrier?" I demanded.

Sam took a swig from the flask before pondering my question. After a brief pause, he locked eyes with me.

"I knew you wouldn't agree to the plan."

Shocked, I asked, "So, you lied to me?"

"No... I just never volunteered the information."

"You tricked me," I said, lowering my head in shame. The more I thought about our actions, the more upset I became. "You killed Chief..."

"He was biting you."

I lifted my head and glared at him. "He was protecting Taya and her newborn cub." As a tear fell from my eye, Sam caught his breath, realizing the hurt I was feeling. He handed the flask over, thinking I could wash away my sorrows with booze. I was in so much pain that I took the flask and drank from it.

"The furrier will be here in the morning, and then we'll find another circus to join."

I sobbed quietly.

"Take another sip."

"No!" I yelled, throwing the flask to the ground. The remaining whiskey spilled out.

Sam stood, becoming upset, but sat down quickly, thinking better of it. He knew not to question my actions.

"Don't you have any remorse? Chief had a wife and a baby on the way," I muttered.

"What's done is done."

I couldn't stop sobbing as I realized that forgiving myself would be impossible. We had committed a wrongdoing, and there was no way to amend it. Nevertheless, I took responsibility for my part and tried to make things right. I stood up and took a deep breath. "I'm going to check on Taya," I muttered.

Leaving Sam alone by the campfire, I wandered into the dimly lit night, lost in my thoughts. When I arrived at Taya's enclosure, I found her huddled protectively with her cub. Full of caution and mistrust, her eyes followed me as I approached.

"I'm not here to hurt you," I assured her gently, lowering myself to meet her eye level. "I'm so sorry for what we've done."

My sorrow burst forth like a dam breaking. The tears flowed, and I sobbed uncontrollably. "I won't let him hurt you. I'll think of something before the furrier comes in the morning."

In response, Taya extended her paw toward me, her body language understanding my grief. There was an unspoken bond in that moment, a silent communication of empathy from a creature I had wronged. The forgiveness in her gesture was unmistakable. It wasn't an absolution of my actions but an acknowledgment of my remorse. It gave me a glimmer of hope, a tiny spark that suggested I might, one day, forgive myself too.

With this newfound sense of purpose, I returned to the campfire, resolved to foil Sam's plan to sell Taya. As I took my seat, Sam remained silent, perhaps sensing the subtle shift in power between us. It was an epiphany, a stark realization that I was no longer a pawn in his game. We were equals, and he could never exert control over me again.

35

AXLE

W E REACHED THE LAGOON and were captivated by the sight before us. Looking across the water, I spotted Bird Island, a natural sanctuary where birds could roost, nest, and breed. The island was densely packed with trees and vegetation, providing cover from predators and harsh weather.

After surveying the pond, I felt relieved and found crossing safe if everyone knew how to swim. Though I wasn't the strongest swimmer, dog paddling came naturally. Marceau and Molly both nodded when I asked if they could swim. Exhaling in relief, I knew getting across the water wouldn't pose a problem.

Leading the way, with Marceau covering our rear, we cautiously entered the lagoon. The cool water felt good against our skin—however, the depth was intimidating, and we had to pay close attention to the floating logs.

As we swam to the island, a growl echoed in the distance. I quickly turned and saw a bear swimming toward us. Panic hit me, and I knew we had to act fast.

"Turn around!" I yelled.

Frightened, Molly froze in the water.

Marceau swam to her, grabbed her, and dragged her to safety.

As I reached the shore behind them, I spun around to find the bear upon us. Our rescue mission had turned into a race for survival.

"Run!" I shouted.

Molly scrambled away and hid behind a large bush while Marceau and I braced ourselves for the imminent attack. I pushed Marceau away, but he stood firmly by my side.

The bear emerged from the water, towering over us. Its teeth bared in a snarl, and the sight of its fangs sent chills through us. I faced the bear with a defiant growl, hoping to intimidate it. However, it didn't back down.

Marceau charged, barking loudly.

Unimpressed by our bravery, the bear delivered a powerful slap. The force of the blow threw Marceau to the ground, rendering him unconscious.

"Marceau!" Molly cried out.

Adrenaline rushed through me as I jumped forward, driven by a strong urge to protect. My paws flew, aimed at the bear's face.

Enraged, the bear swung back with its massive claws extended.

I sidestepped its attack, feeling a rush of wind. Yet, I wasn't quick enough to evade his teeth. Blood gushed from my nose.

I bit back.

The bear roared with rage as my teeth momentarily sank into its flesh.

The fight escalated quickly. We traded blows, neither willing to give in. The bear's paw suddenly hit my head, sending me sprawling to the ground.

As I struggled to regain my senses, terror seized me—the bear was going for Marceau's lifeless body.

Panic overwhelmed me. I leaped forward, but it was too late. The bear clamped down on Marceau and ran away into the darkness.

"Marceau!" Molly screamed.

I stood there, crushed by helplessness and defeat. Grief consumed me, and I collapsed, sorrow pulling me into despair.

Molly's screams continued.

The pain was unbearable, my breathing labored, and I felt my heart ready to give out. I wanted to give in, but I knew I couldn't. "Get up!" I groaned, forcing my trembling legs to stand. Molly needed me now more than ever.

With great effort, I reached her.

When Molly looked up with sorrowful eyes, my heart shattered. I embraced her tightly, enveloping her in love.

36

HARRY

A CREEPY CHITTERING NOISE startled me as we ventured into the murky swamp. I spun around to see two glowing eyes in the darkness. Panicking, I dashed toward my brother, who was unaware of the presence behind us.

Startled by my sudden appearance, he turned around, his brow furrowing.

I pointed toward the glowing eyes.

The chittering noise rose again, louder and more menacing this time.

"It's only a raccoon. It won't hurt you," he murmured.

"I want to go home," I cried.

Seeing my distress, Jett's demeanor softened, surprising me.

"I won't let anything harm you."

I turned back to the raccoon, which chittered again. "It scares me..." I admitted, my voice trembling.

"Close your eyes and take a deep breath."

"What?"

"Do as I say..."

Despite the uncertainty in his words, I complied, closing my eyes and taking a deep breath.

"Now, count to three and exhale," he instructed further.

I counted one, two, three, and exhaled. When I opened my eyes, a newfound sense of calm enveloped me, washing away my panic.

"You see, it's merely your imagination running wild. There's nothing to be afraid of," he murmured, gesturing toward the raccoon.

As I turned back, the raccoon stepped out from the darkness. It stood on its hind legs, striking a pose oddly reminiscent of a human, and extended a paw in our direction—a gesture surprisingly like a wave. Feeling relieved and a bit embarrassed for letting my imagination get the better of me, I lifted my paw in greeting.

The raccoon waved in return.

Jett's patience and understanding made my heart swell with gratitude. "Thank you..." I whispered, feeling a deep appreciation for him.

Lagging behind the others, I thought our journey would continue. However, when I glanced at Jett, he seemed lost in thought. Just as I was about to say we should move on, his voice suddenly erupted into song.

"Don't let worry and fear weigh you down. Remember, I'm right here beside you. Together, as brothers, we'll brave any storm..."

As the words flowed effortlessly from him, everyone stopped and turned in our direction to witness his singing. Excited, they gathered around us.

I was stunned as I watched him. This was my brother, someone I thought I knew well, yet hearing his voice in song felt like discovering him for the first time.

"Life can be a challenge. And yes, there may be dark days. But you'll find the way with bravery and love..." he sang.

As his song ended, applause erupted around us. Jett's face broke into a wide grin, surprised and delighted by the unexpected attention.

Standing beside me, Elsa's eyes sparkled with admiration. "He has a lovely voice," she remarked.

I nodded in agreement.

"Why does he choose to be a bully when he can be so nice?" Elsa asked, genuinely curious.

"He's scared, just like us," I replied. Seeing him truly happy, I realized he had a heart capable of immense love.

As the excitement waned, we continued through the swamp. Suddenly, Morton's urgent cry to slow down halted us again. We turned to see him bent over, taking exaggerated, heaving breaths. His theatrically overstated exhaustion drew amused smiles from all of us.

"I'm exhausted. I can't keep up with your pace," he gasped.

"Poor little guy," Elsa sympathized, trying to stifle a grin. "Of course, you can't. You're smaller than we are."

I watched as she picked him up and placed him on her head. A large grin spread immediately across his face, surprised at her generosity.

"Thank you!" he burst out, his gratitude shining through his earlier fatigue.

"Hold on tight!" Elsa advised.

The roles had reversed, with Elsa now taking on the role of a parent. Her words provided him with a sense of safety and warmth.

As our journey continued, Morton suddenly broke down, bringing us to yet another halt.

"What's troubling you now?" Elsa asked, her voice filled with concern.

Amidst his sobs, Morton struggled to articulate his sorrow. After a moment, he took a deep, shuddering breath and spoke candidly.

"Your kindness has compounded my shame...," he confessed.

A ripple of confusion passed through us, our exchanged glances reflecting our bewilderment.

"It was my job to inform you of Taya and Mischa's whereabouts," Morton admitted. "But I gave in to temptation and stopped for breakfast after returning to the circus. I overindulged and fell asleep," he continued, each word laced with remorse.

"Oh, Morton..." Elsa sighed softly, her voice brimming with compassion as she began to understand his turmoil.

"In my selfishness, I lost sight of what truly mattered. The thought that my actions could cause harm consumes me with guilt."

Elsa raised her trunk gently, soothingly stroking his head.

"What if we're too late?"

"Everything will be fine," Elsa assured him, her voice steady and full of conviction.

"I'll never forgive myself..."

"You made a mistake," she murmured, offering him comfort.

As we continued our journey, Morton wiped away his tears, reassured by the knowledge that he was forgiven.

I saw Jett glancing back at me from the corner of my eye. I returned his look with a grin and quickened my pace.

As I fell into stride beside him, he leaned on me. This small gesture held immense significance—it was his way of saying, without words, that he loved me.

37

MOLLY

A S WE SWAM toward Bird Island, every ripple felt like a wave, and every sound reverberated around me, intensifying my senses. Suddenly, something brushed against my paw, causing me to gasp and turn. Struggling against the darkness, I peered into the depths below, where I identified a familiar shape.

To my horror, Axle had stopped breathing and was rapidly sinking below the water's surface. Panic surged through me, causing my heart to race as I dove toward him. I grabbed him and kicked my legs furiously, propelling us toward the shore. Suddenly, he gasped for air, regaining consciousness.

"We're almost there!" I bellowed. But as the words left my mouth, Axle sank again. Taking a deep breath of fresh air, I dove beneath the water and pulled him back to the surface.

I shouted for him to dog paddle. But when I looked into his eyes, I saw nothing but exhaustion. It was clear he didn't have the strength to move forward.

Tears welled up in my eyes, blurring my vision. My sobs echoed across the lagoon. The thought of losing him became all too real.

"Swim!" I cried out, my voice breaking with desperation.

Axle's front legs started moving.

"We're going to make it," I said, watching his every move. When he halted from sheer exhaustion, I pushed him forward.

As we reached the island, he staggered out of the water and collapsed onto the sand. Gasping for breath, I watched him struggle to get up. His strength had evaporated.

"What are you doing? You need to rest!" I cried out, unable to comprehend his actions. His legs quivered like a newborn fawn, shaking uncontrollably and failing to support his weight.

"Marceau would want us to move on."

I looked at Axle, my heart swelling with sadness. The bandages on his legs had come undone from the bear's attack and the ordeal in the lagoon. He didn't look well, and as a premonition washed over me that he might not return home, I shook the thoughts away.

Witnessing his courage and the will to push forward despite the heavy burden of his pain ignited something within me. I knew I had to hold myself together and help him.

"We'll proceed with caution," I said, standing, ready to face whatever lay ahead with a newfound determination.

As we began our slow walk forward, I moved to stand beside him, aware that his heart might give out at any moment. Axle remained silent—his thoughts consumed by the rescue mission. My mind whirled as I recalled our first meeting. It was astonishing how life could change. I turned to him, "If it weren't for you, I'd still be on the streets."

Axle shook his head in understanding.

"Thank you for saving me."

"You're welcome."

Driven by a desire to keep the connection alive, I ventured further. "You've never talked about a family."

"You mean a wife? Puppies?" he asked, his tone laced with an underlying sorrow.

I signaled my curiosity with a nod.

He turned away then—his gaze clouded with a sadness that spoke volumes. There was someone he held dear, yet circumstances cruelly kept them apart. Even as the silence grew longer, when he finally faced me again, sidestepping my inquiry, his words were a stark reminder of our urgent mission.

"We're running out of time."

In his distant look, I sensed his thoughts drifting to the one he loved. At that moment, a profound realization dawned on me. Though he remained unspoken, it was clear there had never been a wife or puppies. I understood that he directed his love toward someone he could not openly claim as I pieced together his sexuality. Without his confession, I was at a loss for words, unable to offer consolation.

Silently, I followed him, the heaviness of his unspoken sadness resting upon my shoulders. Studying him, I noted how his movements shed their initial stiffness.

In this silent companionship, amidst the shadows of our mission and the ghosts of unspoken truths, I realized the profound bond that connected us. Our shared path, marked by loss, had forged a connection far beyond what we expected.

◆◆◆

We reached the campsite quietly, hiding behind a tree. Axle cautiously extended a branch to observe the carneys lounging in their makeshift encampment.

"They're intoxicated," he muttered under his breath, his voice laced with a mix of relief and concern.

My worry for our safety intensified with each passing second, but Axle, sensing my fear, reassured me with a confident whisper.

"They won't even know we've been here."

With trepidation gripping my heart, I followed Axle, moving cautiously closer to the truck. My pulse raced thunderously in my ears.

Axle advanced with determined strides—his every move purposeful as he surveyed the unsettling scene before us.

As I peered intently into the cage, my gaze settled on Taya and Mischa, both fast asleep. Abruptly, Axle's whisper pierced the enveloping silence.

"Taya!"

His voice, though soft, was enough to jolt her from her slumber.

Upon seeing Axle, Taya's expression swiftly morphed from shock to unbridled joy. Her whisper, laden with happiness and relief, floated back to us.

"I knew you'd come!"

Amid their heartfelt reunion, something else caught my eye—a padlock, imposing and cold, securing the cage firmly. "They've locked the door," I remarked, my voice barely more than a hushed murmur.

A shadow fell over Axle's features as he took in this new hurdle, his brows knitting together in frustration. It was clear his mind was racing, gears turning rapidly as he contemplated our next move, his resolve hardening against the challenge we faced.

"How are we going to release them?"

"Spread the bars," he decided, moving away from Taya's side to stand on his hind legs. He placed his powerful paws against the metal rods, muscles bulging as he exerted himself to their limit to pry them apart. Yet the bars remained unyielding, a silent testament to their fortitude against Axle's desperate efforts.

Inside the cage, the atmosphere filled with tension. Taya, her eyes wide with anxiety, began pacing in a tight pattern.

A moment later, Axle slumped in defeat, his failure clear. Taya looked at him with concern, her tail twitching nervously.

"The carney... has the key around his neck," she whispered, her voice trembling with fear and desperation.

Her revelation redirected our gaze toward the carney's campsite, the weight of her words settling heavily upon us. Axle and I exchanged a look, our minds whirling with potential strategies. The key, so crucial to our plan, now seemed tantalizingly close and distant.

Amid our contemplation, Taya's deep, guttural roar shattered the silence.

"Taya, stop!" Axle urged—his voice strained as he fought to keep panic at bay.

Ignoring his plea, Taya roared again, her voice echoing through the night. Suddenly, a loud "hoot" cut through the air, dampening the intensity of Taya's roars.

Our attention snapped back to the carneys, hearts racing. Sam and Billy-Joe sat up abruptly, their gaze darting in confusion, attempting to pierce the darkness.

38

BOBBI-CAT

I PROPELLED MYSELF FORWARD in a sprint toward the babies, who had just triumphantly arrived at the lagoon's edge under the mistaken belief that they had reached Bird Island. Their infectious enthusiasm swept over me as I hastily scanned the area for any sign of lurking predators. Suddenly, from the periphery of my vision, I caught sight of an alligator gently breaking the surface of the water. It blinked twice—its gaze fixed with an intrigued curiosity before gliding forward silently. A lump formed in my throat as I realized the young ones were unaware of the impending danger.

"We made it!" Mia exclaimed in triumph.

"No, we haven't," Jett countered softly, his voice tinged with disappointment as he gestured across the lagoon. "That's Bird Island!" His revelation brought a sudden shift in the atmosphere.

"How will we get there?" Mia questioned, her voice laced with genuine concern, still oblivious to the perilously simple solution before them.

"We're going to swim," Jett declared.

"Why not use the bridge?" Morton questioned.

"Because it's on the other side of the island."

"It'll be safer!" Morton stated.

Jett shook his head. "We don't have time for that. We're swimming!"

"Are you nuts?" Morton shouted.

"What about the alligators?" Harry added quietly, his voice barely above a whisper, as he warily surveyed the lagoon.

At that moment, as if sensing our collective attention, the alligator silently slipped beneath the water's surface, vanishing and leaving an uneasy quiet in its wake.

The mere thought of swimming made Morton struggle to catch his breath. His exaggerated movements were impossible to ignore. As his breathing grew more labored, he clutched his forehead with dramatic flair before collapsing to the ground.

"I'm a bad swimmer!" he wailed.

Ignoring Morton's theatrics, Jett reassured his brother, "There are no alligators in the lagoon."

"How do you know that?" Harry questioned—curiosity evident in his voice.

"Watch this!" Jett murmured as he picked up a small rock and threw it into the lagoon. "If there's anything out there, it'll surface."

The stone hit the water and sank quickly.

As everyone held their breath in anticipation of something surfacing, seconds passed with nothing happening.

"See... Believe me now?" Jett stated.

"Okay..." Harry responded.

"Let's go!" Jett directed, urging everyone forward.

As they moved toward the water's edge, Harry glanced across the lagoon one last time and saw the alligator surfacing. His voice caught in his throat as he tried to shout out a warning, but because of fear, it was inaudible. Receiving no response, he pointed and shouted again, successfully grabbing everyone's attention this time.

"Alligator!"

Everyone turned to see the gator opening its mouth in their direction. As it abruptly snapped its jaws shut, thunder rumbled overhead, and a flash of lightning illuminated the night sky, further terrifying the group. The overly dramatic Morton wheezed again before finally collapsing onto the sand, fainting for real. Knowing it was time to reveal myself, I shouted to get everyone's attention and ran toward them.

Everyone turned, surprised to see me emerge from the bushes, but their focus immediately shifted back to the alligator approaching them. As it made its way toward the shore, the alligator stood high on all fours, its tail weaving back and forth.

Morton regained consciousness just in time to see the reptile emerging from the water. He sighed loudly and fainted once again. Elsa came to his rescue, snatching him up with her trunk, and retreated with the others.

To my surprise, Jett and Harry stayed bravely, confronting the approaching predator.

"Get back!" I yelled.

As the alligator crawled toward them, Jett screamed, turned, and ran away, leaving Harry alone.

Everyone cried out to run away.

The alligator found amusement in their panic. A low chuckle resonated from its throat, and its eyes gleamed with mischief as it advanced.

The alligator, keenly observing Harry's fear, flashed a sinister, toothy grin. She spoke, her voice surprisingly feminine yet chillingly contrasted against her intimidating appearance.

"Well, aren't you just a little morsel?" she teased, her tone thick with malicious delight as if savoring the taste of her words. "Just a lion cub—I could swallow you whole. You'd make a rather delectable treat."

Upon hearing the alligator's menacing words, Harry's already heightened fear surged to an unprecedented peak. His body trembled uncontrollably, racked with terror.

"Fortunately for you, I've just had my dinner," the alligator proclaimed.

Crouching down to appear menacing, Harry let out a high-pitched squeak that bore no resemblance to a roar. Shockingly, this elicited guttural laughter from the alligator.

"Leave us alone!" Harry shouted defiantly, lunging forward to scare the alligator away.

"Je-Jett, do something!" Luca cried out in a panic, his voice piercing the night, but Jett continued to retreat, too petrified to intervene.

"We mean you no harm," Harry attempted to reason with the alligator.

"This is my territory, and you're trespassing," the alligator growled back, her voice thunderous and menacing. She opened her mouth wide to reveal a terrifying array of razor-sharp teeth, each capable of inflicting unimaginable pain.

I could see the alligator preparing to strike. Just as I rushed forward to pull him back, a thunderous boom echoed in the distance, signaling the start of a torrential downpour. The wind howled as it accompanied the rain.

I stopped dead in my tracks as Harry faced the alligator unflinchingly. Any chance for my intervention had slipped away.

"I'm a ferocious lion," he declared, his newfound boldness surprising us, his voice cutting through the stormy night.

Surprised by Harry's sudden display of courage, the alligator momentarily faltered. She snapped her jaw shut with a menacing clack and reared onto her hind legs, towering over him with a looming presence.

"Oh, really?" she taunted, her voice oozing with amusement and mockery.

Suddenly, a group of alligators emerged from the murky water, crawling onto the shore with chilling precision.

"I'm asking you kindly. Please, let us pass." Harry pleaded, his sniffles now loud sobs that filled the night air with despair.

"I can't do that!" The alligator replied, saliva dripping from its mouth.

"Why?"

The reptile grinned, pointing at the alligators inching closer. "They're hungry," she remarked.

"YOU WON'T MAKE A MEAL OUT OF US!" Harry yelled defiantly.

In a breathtaking instant, Harry dropped into a crouch and propelled himself forward. A fierce roar erupted from the depths of his being, not the usual squeak but a thunderous declaration of courage that shook the ground beneath them.

The female alligator, caught off guard by the unexpected ferocity, stumbled back onto the sandy shore. The group of alligators hesitated in stunned disbelief, reluctant to move any closer.

We watched with bated breath, hearts racing, curious about what would unfold next. As the alligator regained her footing, she offered a maternal smile, adding an unexpected twist to the evening's events.

"I knew you could do it!" she exclaimed, her tone now warm and encouraging, starkly contrasting to her earlier malevolence.

Harry sat back on his haunches, sniffling loudly, a mixture of relief and residual fear coursing through him.

"My name's Sadie, and this is my family," the alligator introduced, gesturing toward the other reptiles with motherly pride.

A thunderous boom rumbled in the distance, startling everyone.

"There's no need to fear the storm or us. Neither will harm you."

"Then why did you frighten me?" Harry asked, raising his paw to shield himself from the falling raindrops.

"It was a lesson. You needed to learn how to defend yourself."

"You were never going to hurt me?"

"No," Sadie reassured. "I would never harm you or your friends."

As if on cue, the dark clouds overhead parted, and the rain softened. Moonlight broke through, and Sadie looked up with a smile, watching the storm diminish.

"The storm is passing," she said.

I sighed with relief, assured that everything would be fine. As I sat down, a lightning bolt streaked across the sky, startling everyone.

"The storm's not over!" Mia exclaimed—her voice tinged with panic.

Sadie lowered her head, pondering deeply as she searched for the words to explain the storm's gradual passing. After a moment, she lifted her head and smiled reassuringly.

"When you see a flash of lightning, start counting the seconds until you hear the thunder," she explained.

The babies tilted their heads, their expressions puzzled as they tried to grasp the meaning behind her comment.

"It'll tell you the storm's distance," Sadie clarified as another flash of lightning lit up the sky. "Start counting," she instructed. "One Mississippi, two Mississippi, three Mississippi..."

The babies counted along, "Four Mississippi, five Mississippi..."

As the distant rumble of thunder interrupted them, Sadie exclaimed, "Stop counting. For every five seconds between lightning and thunder, the storm is one mile away."

"I get it!" Mia shouted.

"I get-get it, too!" Luca exclaimed, jumping excitedly.

Smiling at the babies, I turned toward Sadie as she gestured for her family to gather around. Moments later, she surprised everyone and hollered, "Hit it, boys!"

As the alligators lined up, they began an unexpected performance. One reptile stood behind a rock, using its foot to drum a beat, while the others clapped and stomped in rhythm. Then, suddenly, Sadie started singing a fun and catchy tune.

"When the storm clouds gather, and the sky turns gray, we don't duck and cover. When lightning strikes, we dance, dance, dance…"

No longer afraid of the storm, everyone began leaping and twirling in the rain. I couldn't resist joining in. It was a magical moment—even Morton, who had felt faint before, moved to the rhythm.

"Under stormy skies, together we'll sway. Amid the chaos, our spirits will fly away…"

As the last notes of the melody faded into the night, the rain stopped, and the once-raging storm came to a standstill.

Sadie approached the group, stood, and extended her front legs in a gesture of goodwill. "Now, how may I help you?" she asked, her voice filled with genuine concern.

Elsa took the lead and stepped forward to explain, "We need to cross the lagoon."

"Well, that's a simple task," Sadie responded, her tone bright and confident. "We'll take you there!" She smiled, gesturing everyone toward the shoreline.

However, Morton appeared visibly anxious. His voice trembled as he voiced his concerns.

"It's pitch black out there. We won't be able to see a thing," he protested.

To everyone's surprise, Sadie took a deep breath and whistled, which caused Morton to cover his ears.

As the group stood, shrouded in the night's darkness, a sudden burst of light caught their attention. Within seconds, a lightning bug fluttered toward them, its body emitting a soft, luminous glow that lit up the area.

To everyone's surprise, the tiny insect landed on Morton's nose. The sight of the glowing bug perched on his snout caused him to freeze, his eyes wide with awe and wonder.

A warm, ethereal light bathed Morton's face as the insect flickered on and off. This unexpected spectacle filled him with an indescribable sense of joy.

"Hello there!" Morton greeted—his voice filled with excitement. His eyes remained fixed on the bug, mesmerized by its hypnotic glow.

"It's so amazing!" Mia murmured as she gazed upon the enchanting insect.

Sadie gestured everyone toward the lined-up alligators, half in and half out of the water, eagerly waiting for passengers.

With his newfound friend, the lightning bug, Morton ran and perched himself atop the first alligator. Then, he beckoned everyone to follow suit with an enthusiastic wave.

Jett and Harry clambered onto the second alligator, and Luca jumped on the third one.

Meanwhile, Elsa and Mia, who were too large to ride on a reptile's back, made their way through the water.

With a playful twinkle in her eyes, Elsa plunged her long trunk into the lagoon and sucked up water, causing her cheeks to balloon slightly. Then, she lifted her trunk and released the water in a spectacular spray. The water arced over everyone, and the droplets glimmered in the soft glow of the lightning bug, creating a mesmerizing spectacle of dancing lights.

The refreshing mist caused an outbreak of delighted squeals and laughter from everyone.

Despite being drenched, the group couldn't help but feel a sense of excitement and anticipation as they continued their journey, led by Morton and his trusty companion, the lightning bug.

I ran toward the last alligator, understanding that swimming was not my thing and that getting wet was my least favorite thing. As I climbed onto its back and sat, I breathed a deep sigh of relief, acknowledging that everyone was safe and in good hands.

At that moment, as I sat surrounded by these reptilian creatures, Sadie's kindness and loving nature truly dawned on me. As I came to this realization, I couldn't help but think that my initial thoughts about alligators were wrong. To my surprise, they, too, could be friendly creatures, a thought that brought a smile to my face and filled me with newfound admiration.

39

HARRY

AS WE RODE on the alligator's back, following Morton and the lightning bug through the darkness, I noticed Jett lost in thought. He lowered his head, and I could tell something was troubling him. Concerned, I asked, "What's wrong?"

Slowly, he lifted his head, and I saw his eyes were moist with tears. He was upset and bothered by something. After he wiped his eyes, he mustered up the courage to tell me what was on his mind.

"I left you in danger. What if something happened?" he said, his voice shaking with emotion.

I reassured him, "Nothing happened. Sadie's a nice alligator."

Jett lowered his head again, overcome with emotion. When he looked up, tears were streaming down his cheeks.

"I haven't been a good brother," he admitted. "Everyone thinks I'm a bully. I act tough, so no one sees how weak I am."

"We're all scared... It's okay to show your emotions."

I hugged him tightly, overwhelmed with compassion. "You're my brother. I love and understand you. You don't have to pretend to be someone else."

At that moment, I noticed a spark in his eyes. He finally understood that we loved him, weaknesses and all.

We continued along our journey, and eventually, the darkness lifted, revealing the glow of the carney's campfire. It was a reminder that no matter how dark life may seem, there's always a light at the end of the tunnel.

40

MORTON

L EADING THE WAY through the darkness, I spotted the carney's campfire. Excitedly, I began shouting, "There! Over there!"

I directed the alligators to the shore, and everyone disembarked. Unfortunately, I lost my balance and fell, landing face-first in the sand.

Lifting my head, I was surprised to see everyone laughing. My initial reaction was anger, but then I realized they were laughing with me—not at me. A grin spread across my face, and I joined in, sharing a spontaneous moment of joy with everyone.

As the alligators returned to the water, except for Sadie, we gathered around her.

Harry stepped forward, saying, "We wouldn't have made it without you. Thank you..."

Sadie smiled warmly. "You're welcome. I'm so proud of you…"

"He's braver than me," Jett admitted, showing a surprising moment of vulnerability.

As Harry grinned at his brother's comment, Sadie smiled, knowing it was time to say goodbye.

"It's been a pleasure meeting all of you. Be safe on your journey."

We waved goodbye.

Before departing, Sadie leaned in and whispered to Harry. I listened intently—her words filled my heart with joy.

"You're a special boy. Your love and tenderness shine through. Always remain true to who you are…"

Harry hugged Sadie.

She returned his embrace, planting a gentle kiss on his head. As she pulled away, she waved goodbye and walked into the water. We watched as she gradually sank beneath the surface, vanishing into the depths.

Once the excitement settled, our journey to find Axle, Marceau, and Molly continued. Wanting to save time, Bobbi-cat suggested we ride on Elsa's back to reach our destination.

Elsa's excitement was evident as she lowered herself to the ground, inviting us all to climb aboard, ready to carry us forward.

Despite my initial trepidation, I giggled as we crowded onto Elsa's back, holding each other tightly to avoid falling off. As Elsa rose, my heart pounded with fear, but as we gained height, I quickly realized this was just another adventure.

With each passing moment, the journey on Elsa's back became more exhilarating, and I felt my fear melting away as I took in the stunning landscape around us.

Mia's joyful shouts echoed through the air, and I joined her, shouting, "WEEEEEEE!" in sheer exhilaration. It was a moment of pure bliss and excitement.

In an unexpected twist, Elsa suddenly lifted her trunk and released a mighty trumpet, boldly announcing our presence. A fleeting worry crossed my mind that the carneys might hear, but the sheer joy of the ride quickly overshadowed any concerns.

41

BILLY-JOE

AMIDST MY ALCOHOL-INDUCED haze, the sudden trumpeting of an elephant jolted me upright. I blinked, unsure if my mind was playing tricks on me. Desperate for confirmation, I nudged Sam and asked if he had heard it, too. He motioned for silence just as another trumpet blast filled the air, his expression twisting into bewilderment and disbelief. I kept my eyes on him, anticipating some sort of explanation.

"There are no elephants on the island."

"I just heard one..." I pressed.

Annoyed, Sam took off his cap and smacked me with it. "We're on Bird Island. You're a numbskull. Birds only!"

I quickly covered my head and stood, glaring at him fiercely. "Stop hitting me!"

His eyes widened in response to my anger.

Calming down, he replaced his cap and suggested I check on Taya and Mischa, admitting he'd had too much to drink.

As I moved forward, my legs gave way. I realized I was just as intoxicated and sat down.

"What are you doing?" he asked, puzzled.

"I'm drunk, too!" I confessed.

Sam appeared lost in thought as we sat together, enveloped in silence. I found myself savoring the tranquility, choosing not to disturb his contemplation.

Suddenly, a spark of realization lit up Sam's face, transforming his expression into one of sheer delight. With a grin, he broke the silence with an excited exclamation.

"It's an African Grey Parrot!"

His unexpected revelation surprised me.

He explained how the Parrot could mimic the sound of an elephant.

"That can't be right," I argued. "That had to be an elephant. Are you losing your mind?"

Just as Sam was about to retaliate with his cap again, I stood my ground and met his gaze sternly, causing him to sit back down and reconsider his actions.

42

AXLE

HEARING THE TRUMPETING sound of an elephant, I quickly turned my head. To my astonishment, it was Elsa. I could hear the unmistakable giggles of the babies in the background. Turning to Molly with disbelief, I realized they had followed us.

At that moment, Taya released a deafening roar, trying to capture their attention.

Despite my efforts to calm her, she continued bellowing, signaling our location to the little ones.

Holding my breath, I hoped the carneys were still in a drunken stupor and hadn't heard her. Soon, Elsa came charging toward us, my eyes widening at the babies joyously riding on her back.

When Elsa finally saw us, she skidded to a halt and gracefully lowered herself to the ground. The little ones slid off her back and ambled toward us.

Initially speechless, I found my voice and said, "You shouldn't have followed us."

"We were worried about you," Elsa replied, her gaze shifting toward Harry as he slipped and fell off her back.

Harry got up, flashing a grin.

Suppressing a smile, I knew I needed to impress upon them the danger of their decision. "This is a hazardous place," I stated, sounding as adult-like as possible.

"But-but Axle..." Luca interjected disbelief in his voice. "We came to help you!"

I took a deep breath and realized gratitude was in order. "Thank you, everyone."

"You're welcome!" Mia exclaimed cheerfully, but her expression quickly shifted to confusion. "Where's Marceau?"

Molly inhaled deeply, the harsh reality of Marceau's passing hitting her hard. I gasped as well, dreading the explanation of his death.

"Axle?" Elsa murmured—her voice heavy with seriousness.

"We lost him," I whispered.

The babies looked on in confusion.

"Lost him? Like, he's missing?" Harry's voice quivered with uncertainty.

I shook my head, my heart aching. "He's dead. A bear attacked us."

"Dead?" Harry repeated, his voice faint.

"He's gone forever," I confirmed.

Their gasps of shock and disbelief echoed around us, breaking my heart as I saw their innocent faces twisted in sorrow. Attempting to offer comfort, I added, "He's in a peaceful place now."

Luca nodded, a flicker of understanding in his eyes. "He's with Chief!"

I nodded back, my throat tightening at his realization. "Yes, Luca. They're together now."

Turning away, I caught sight of Mia hugging Molly tightly. Despite her young age, Mia seemed mature beyond her years. I admired her strength and resilience in such a difficult moment.

Though it pained me to think about Marceau, I knew we couldn't dwell on his passing. With a heavy heart, I turned back to everyone, my voice now steady and clear. "We need to get the padlock key from around the carney's neck."

"Oh, Axle!" Elsa interrupted—her voice filled with hope. "We don't need a key. I can pry open the bars..."

"I've already tried," I responded.

Overflowing with excitement, she pleaded to give it a try. She believed her trunk and strong body could succeed where I had failed. Even though I had my doubts, Elsa's determination convinced me to give her a chance.

As Elsa reached the cage, a flock of Black Heron birds flew overhead, chirping loudly. They drew our attention as they flew toward the carney's campsite.

Watching intently, I saw Frank and George landing gracefully on a tree branch. Within moments, George leaned forward with curiosity and listened to the carneys below. Yet, his concentration was shattered when Frank let out a groan, clutching his stomach with a pained expression.

"My belly's upset..." he muttered.

Out of nowhere, a loud, prolonged "toot" resonated through the air.

"Oh dear!" Frank blurted out—his cheeks flushed with embarrassment.

George's eyes widened in disbelief as he quickly covered his beak with his wing, a visible cloud of gas drifting around them.

"Those cherries we ate did a number on me. I need to… and fast!" Frank confessed—his voice tinged with desperation.

Another lengthy, resonant fart followed, causing him to wrinkle his beak in mortification as he frantically fanned the air with his wing, desperately trying to dissipate the offending odor.

George shook his head in disbelief, then turned to the flock of birds and gestured to listen closely.

"I have a plan…"

Unsure of what they were scheming, I turned my attention back to Elsa. She had already reached the cage and was now pulling the bars apart. Her strength made the task seem effortless. I placed my paw on her shoulder, expressing my gratitude.

"You're welcome!" Elsa beamed, clearly pleased to have been of help.

"You did it!" Jett shouted—his voice filled with excitement.

Elsa turned toward Jett and smiled, acknowledging his appreciation of her size and strength.

Turning my gaze, I saw Taya lifting Mischa by the scruff of her neck and carrying her toward the spread bars. When Mischa emerged from the opening, I caught her securely.

Taya roared with joy, grateful that her baby was safe.

I stepped back to allow Taya to exit—however, there was a problem. She couldn't squeeze through.

"The opening's too small!" Taya announced anxiously, peering outward.

"Let me try again!" Elsa announced.

Taya stepped back into the cage.

Elsa began pulling the bars apart, taking matters into her own hands. Sweat beaded on her forehead as she exerted every ounce of strength, attempting to widen the gap, yet the bars refused to budge.

"You're doing great. I'm so proud of you," I consoled, trying to offer encouragement amidst her struggles.

Elsa continued to pull at the bars.

"It won't budge any further. What are we going to do?" she asked, her frustration noticeable.

While I tried to calm her, footsteps suddenly filled the air behind us.

"Someone's coming!" Molly shouted.

"Take Mischa and run!" Taya yelled from within the cage, her pacing a clear sign of anxiety.

Everyone scattered, taking cover in the brush.

Peering out, I saw Sam staggering in drunkenness toward the cage. Upon seeing the gaping hole, he scratched his head in confusion but noted it was too small for Taya to escape. Then he checked the padlock, shaking it to ensure it was secure.

Above him, a squawk erupted.

He stopped fiddling with the lock just in time to see George swooping toward him. Instinctively, he ducked, trying to protect himself.

"Shoo... Go away!" he shouted.

George flew past unscathed.

As Sam stood up, he rolled his eyes and muttered, "Crazy bird."

Another loud squawk echoed above.

Looking up, Sam saw Frank diving toward him.

"Bombs away!" Frank called out as he swooped down, releasing his bowels.

Sam's eyes widened in horror as he saw the excrement hurtling toward him.

It hit his face with a splat.

"AHHHHHHH..." Sam groaned loudly, wiping his face and flicking the mess away.

I couldn't help but giggle at the sight. Glancing at Jett, I noticed he was looking at Elsa with a guilty expression.

"Elsa?" he murmured.

"Yes, Jett?" she responded.

"What I said about your weight was wrong. I'm sorry that I hurt your feelings. I realize my mistake now," he admitted, remorse coloring his tone.

"Oh, Jett…"

"Can you forgive me?" he asked, hopeful for reconciliation.

Elsa took a deep breath, and a single tear fell from her eye. Her emotions surged upon hearing Jett's apology.

"Yes, I forgive you," she whispered, leaning into him. Her weight almost crushed him, but he pushed back against her with a smile.

"Thank you, Elsa."

My heart swelled, seeing Jett being polite and caring. His bullying persona was changing, and he was becoming a better cub.

From the carney's campsite, Billy-Joe's screams echoed in the distance. Everyone, including Sam, turned to see what was happening.

As Sam ran toward the campsite, I left my hiding place and followed him. When I arrived, I saw the flock of Heron birds attacking Billy-Joe. He was on the ground, kicking his feet and flailing his hands.

"Help me! Help me!" he cried.

As Sam tried to shoo the birds away, they turned on him. He fell to the ground, trying to protect himself. By this time, everyone was standing behind me, their eyes wide with astonishment.

Just then, an owl flew by and dived toward Sam. I watched the carney's eyes widen in fear at the bird's descent. He screamed aloud, covering his face.

"Noooo…"

The owl extended his claws and snatched the key.

"Give that back to me!" Sam shouted, reaching out in vain as the owl escaped his grasp and flew away.

As the owl soared gracefully toward Taya's cage, we chased after him, our hearts brimming with excited glee.

With a sly grin, he landed beside the cage and held up the key.

"Is this what you're looking for?" he teased.

Overjoyed at the sight of the owl, Morton ran forward, exclaiming, "Ollie! Ollie! You came back and saved the day!"

Handing Mischa over to Molly, I reached for the key.

As Ollie dropped it into my paw, I felt a sudden pain in my chest. I jerked back, and the key fell to the ground.

Everyone gasped in surprise.

Taking a deep breath, I waited for the pain to subside. Once it faded, I turned to the babies, knowing it was wrong to lie to them, but I couldn't admit my heart was faltering. Taya still needed to be released, and the babies needed to get home.

"Axle?" Molly murmured—her voice laced with concern.

I turned to her, realizing she knew my heart was weakening. I shook my head, silently pleading with her to keep quiet.

Molly's expression showed she understood.

"Clumsy me!" I exclaimed, trying to deflect their concern as I picked up the key. I walked over and unlocked the cage, opening the door.

Taya burst from the cage, her leap igniting a chorus of delight from the babies. Her triumphant roar reverberated as the carneys, suddenly aware of her escape, sprinted toward us.

Taya charged with a thunderous roar.

The carneys, gripped by sheer panic, stopped their pursuit, shrieked, and stumbled over each other in a mad dash to the truck.

They rushed inside, slamming the doors in a frantic haste.

Sam's hands shook violently as he fumbled with the keys, his heart pounding as Taya loomed at the driver's side window.

"Hurry!" Billy-Joe yelled, his voice cracking with urgency.

Finally, Sam managed to jam the key into the ignition, and the engine roared to life. They tore into the night as everyone cheered, celebrating the triumphant moment.

As the truck disappeared into the shadows, a loud backfire from its engine startled the flock of Herons, sending them skyward. As they pursued the retreating vehicle, their wings cut through the night air with relentlessly.

43

BILLY-JOE

SITTING IN THE TRUCK'S passenger seat, disbelief mounted as bird droppings splattered onto the windshield. What began as a slow trickle swiftly turned into a deluge, obscuring the road ahead. I glanced at Sam, who seemed equally bewildered by the situation.

"Turn on the wipers!" I shouted—my voice laced with panic.

Sam complied, but the wipers only smeared the mess.

Dread washed over me as I turned to him, yelling, "Where's the fluid?" We were driving blind.

Sam fiddled with the knob, but nothing happened.

Leaning forward, I squinted through the droppings and saw the bridge gate looming ahead. Panicked, I shouted for him to plow through it.

Sam let out a shriek that could wake the dead as the truck smashed into the gate, sending it splashing into the water.

"Stay on the bridge!" I yelled as we veered dangerously close to the edge. Just as it seemed, we might plunge into the depths below—a splash of water cleared the windshield of bird droppings.

Grateful for the sudden clarity, Sam regained control and sped into the darkness.

Guilt and regret consumed my mind as we continued in silence. I couldn't shake the feeling that getting involved in Sam's schemes had been a colossal mistake. Looking through the rear window, I saw the flock of Herons on the bridge, seemingly high-fiving one another.

As my mind wandered back to my predicament, worry churned within me about Chief's wife and unborn pup. Nausea washed over me as I faced forward, staring into the darkness. I realized that while I couldn't change the past, I had the power to alter the future. Determined to make things right, I resolved to turn us in and face the consequences of our actions.

44

BOBBI-CAT

AS WE HEADED back to the circus grounds, Molly took charge of the babies while I stayed by Axle's side, observing his unsteady steps. Audubon Park was alive with fireflies, their gentle glow guiding us through the encroaching darkness. A distant roar echoed as we passed the zoo, breaking the silence.

Luca's eyes sparkled with excitement as he sprinted toward Axle, exclaiming, "Take me home! You're the only one who can!"

I stepped in, knowing the journey would be too taxing for Axle in his current state. I tried to convince Luca to wait until tomorrow, hoping Sofia would take him, but disappointment clouded his face.

"Please take me home…"

Despite my efforts, Axle reassured Luca that he would. Molly and I exchanged concerned looks, silently acknowledging Axle's frailty. Luca bounced with exhilaration—his energy infectious. Suddenly, he paused, his joy tempered by the realization that he had to bid farewell to his friends.

"I'm going to miss everyone!"

Jett stepped forward in a moment of vulnerability, his voice trembling sincerely.

"I'm going to miss you, too," he admitted, the weight of his words hanging in the air.

Ever the optimist, Luca promised they'd see each other again.

Despite the emotional exchange, Axle reminded everyone of the harsh reality—the circus was leaving town at dawn, marking this farewell as final.

"We'll never see each other again," Jett murmured.

With a hopeful lilt, Luca insisted, "The circus will return… It-it's not goodbye!"

Hesitant at first, Jett stood on his hind legs, wanting to hug his friend, overcoming his reservations.

"Hugs are good!" Luca encouraged, breaking through Jett's reluctance.

In a rush of emotion, Jett embraced Luca, the hug lasting long enough to convey what words could not.

"I will always think of you," Luca whispered, pulling away.

Jett nodded, feeling the moment's heaviness, while the other babies chimed in with their goodbyes.

Axle stepped forward, silently signaling that it was time to leave.

Luca glanced back one final time, his voice wavering with emotion.

"Good-Goodbye!"

His words set off a ripple of emotion, causing everyone to well up. As Luca and Axle walked into the darkness, Molly and I gathered everyone to rest until he returned.

45

AXLE

I LIMPED ALONGSIDE LUCA, battling waves of dizziness that threatened to overwhelm me. Despite the urge to lie down and rest, my determination to get Luca home kept me moving. When I glanced over at him, his sorrowful eyes met mine.

"Are you okay?" he asked, sensing my struggle.

Forcing a smile, I lied, assuring him I was fine.

A lone lightning bug flickered, illuminating our path until we reached the zoo's entrance. As the night wrapped around us, the haunting cries of animals pierced the silence. I could feel Luca's unease growing beside me.

"I'm scared," Luca whispered.

"I'll protect you," I assured him, concealing my apprehension as we ventured toward the safari exhibit. Suddenly, a chilling screech erupted behind us, and we spun around, our hearts racing with fear of the unknown.

"What was that?" Luca gasped.

Holding my breath, I gazed into the darkness. Moments later, a pale brown monkey with a pink face and a long tail emerged, charging at us. Luca and I instinctively stepped back.

The monkey halted and rose onto its hind legs.

I told Luca it was a Rhesus Macaque and advised him to stay close. My eyes remained locked on the monkey, attentive to its every move.

"Who goes there?" demanded the monkey.

"My name's Axle," I replied, trying to steady my voice. I couldn't tell if he was dangerous or simply curious. As it stepped forward, it locked eyes on Luca, studying him intently.

"You! The Zebra..." he pointed. "Do I know you?" it asked, its eyes narrowing, trying to place him.

Luca instinctively retreated behind me.

"What's your name?" the monkey probed.

Luca remained silent—his voice caught in his throat.

I stepped in, answering softly, "His name's Luca."

Recognition sparked in the monkey's eyes. It let out a screech that echoed through the zoo, startling a flock of sleeping birds.

"Luca!" it cried, a grin spreading across its face. The monkey bounced from foot to foot with contagious energy. "I almost didn't recognize you—you've grown so much!"

Luca hesitantly peeked out from behind me, his initial fear melting into a mix of surprise and curiosity. "You remember me?" he asked, awe evident in his wide eyes.

"Of course I do!" The monkey relied warmly. "Welcome home!"

I watched as Luca's eyes filled with tears, the reality of his return washing over him. Luca turned to me and murmured, "I'm home, Axle. I'm home…"

I nodded, feeling the warmth of the moment enveloping us.

"I'm finally home…" he repeated, pinching himself to ensure this wasn't a dream.

"You're not dreaming…" the monkey assured, its grin wide and genuine, sharing his happiness.

A smile broke across Luca's face, and he began to sing.

"I never thought… this day would come. I'm home. So many nights, I felt alone. I'm home. I'm home…"

A troop of monkeys emerged from the shadows, their joyous cries blending with Luca's song as they circled in jubilant celebration.

"Look at me… I'm home. I'm home…"

As the song ended, the monkeys enveloped us in their embrace.

After the welcome home excitement faded, the monkeys, our lively guides, led us through the zoo to the safari exhibit. They leaped from branch to branch, beckoning us forward with lively gestures, their tails swinging to the pulse of our shared excitement.

46

ELSA

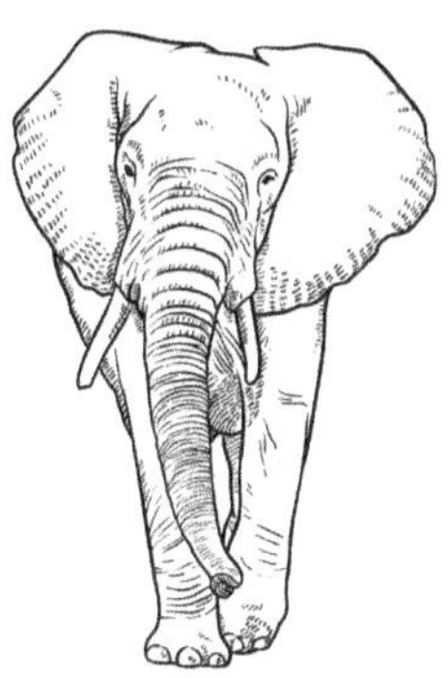

UNDER THE VAST canopy of the "Tree of Life," I watched Molly grieving. I exchanged a glance with Mia—we both felt the need to console her. As we approached, the moonlight filtered through the leaves, casting comforting shadows over us.

Settling beside Molly, I could feel the raw intensity of her pain. When her eyes met mine, they were filled with loss and longing.

"Is there anything we can do to make you feel better?" I asked softly.

"Having you here helps. Thanks," she replied, her words barely above a whisper. Her gratitude was quiet but genuine, and I could tell that just being there offered her some comfort.

"I know how much you loved him."

"I thought my dream of having a family was coming true," she confessed, her words lingering in the air.

"I'm so sorry..." Mia whispered, her voice thick with emotion as she took Molly's paw, tears streaming down her face.

As we lay together beneath the tree, my thoughts wandered to Axle. I was worried about him—he hadn't looked well when he left with Luca, which left me uneasy. Everything felt heavy—Marceau was gone, Molly was heartbroken, and I couldn't stop thinking about my mom, knowing she was worried about me.

Noticing my concern, Taya, nursing Mischa, softly said, "Life is filled with happiness and sorrow. Be strong..."

All I could do was nod. Growing up and facing life's challenges was tough. Turning back to Molly, I wrapped my trunk around her, hoping she would find peace in my embrace, just as I found comfort in my mother's.

As the babies and Morton slept, Molly, Mia, and I remained together, enveloped in each other's presence. Molly's journey through grief was beginning, but I knew that with us by her side, it was a path she wouldn't walk alone.

47

LUCA

AS WE STEPPED into the Safari exhibit, my heart skipped a beat, overwhelmed by anticipation and hope. The herd, my family, was there to greet us, but my mother was not among them. "Wh-where's my mother?" I asked urgently, my voice tinged with desperation.

An elder zebra, her coat marked with the wisdom and experiences of a lifetime, stepped forward with gentle grace. Her kind and understanding eyes met mine as she spoke softly, explaining that my absence had deeply saddened my mother. Each day, she would stand at the edge of the safari exhibit, her eyes scanning the zoo, hoping to catch a glimpse of my return.

I couldn't bear the thought of her sorrow any longer. "Please take me to her," I pleaded, my voice filled with urgency and longing.

The herd set off to fulfill my request, and Axle and I hurried after them. As I glanced back, I noticed Axle lagging behind. Unwilling to leave him, I shouted for the herd to slow down.

"Keep going. I'm right behind you," Axle called out, determination in his voice as he pushed himself to keep up.

As we neared a large tree, I spotted my mom. Her eyes were brimming with tears, her loneliness evident even from a distance. Turning to Axle, I felt excited, "I see her!" I exclaimed—my voice filled with a newfound hope.

As we approached, my mom's eyes scanned the herd, a flicker of confusion crossing her face. That was until Axle stepped forward with a reassuring smile.

"Your son is home," he announced warmly, stepping aside to reveal me standing there.

For a moment, she stood frozen, caught in disbelief. But then, joy erupted from her as she shouted my name. Her voice, a melody of jubilation and relief, filled the air as she raced toward me, her front legs open, ready to envelop me in the comforting warmth of her embrace.

"Mama!" I shouted back. Everything felt right again as she held me.

The herd gathered around us.

I stood with my mom, feeling happy and loved by my family. But as the excitement began to wane, Axle stepped forward, his eyes shadowed by sadness.

"Axle?" I asked, sensing his departure. I stepped away from my mom, my heart heavy with the looming farewell.

"I have to take the others home..." Axle said softly.

I nodded, understanding him. "Thank you!" I said, my voice overflowing with gratitude for everything he had done.

"True friends are never apart, no matter how far they are," he assured me.

"You took care of me," I said. "I think of you as a father..."

"Oh, Luca," Axle replied warmly, his eyes shining with love and pride. "And you are like a son to me. A son I never had. I hope your life is full of happiness. Know that I, and everyone at the circus, love you. You brought us so much joy."

I rested my head against him, savoring the moment.

He pulled back, tears glistening in his eyes.

I watched as he raised his paw one last time, a silent goodbye, before turning to leave. I sat, tears streaming freely down my face, watching him walk away.

My mother came over, her presence a comforting reminder of the love surrounding me. She stood beside me, understanding the depth of my sadness without a word spoken. I leaned into her, seeking solace in her warmth, watching until Axle disappeared completely.

When he was gone, we returned to the tree and were together again in the calm of our home. Together, we settled back into the rhythm of our lives, surrounded by the enduring love of our herd.

48

MOLLY

I LIFTED MY HEAD as Axle returned, my heart swelling with a bittersweet sadness upon seeing how much he had aged during his short absence. The little ones, sensing his return, awoke from their slumber. They stretched and prepared to stand, eager to go home. However, in a moment that tugged at my heart, Axle collapsed beneath the "Tree of Life," overcome by exhaustion.

"Aren't we going home now?" Elsa asked, her youthful curiosity prompting questions about the sudden pause.

I gently knelt beside her, explaining with as much calm as I could muster, "Axle needs to rest before we can begin our journey."

"Is he all right?" Mia chimed in, her voice tinged with worry and concern for Axle.

I shook my head slowly, the unspoken understanding passing through the group. Their eyes filled with concern as Axle let out a long, drawn-out moan, settling his weary head onto his front paws.

"Oh, no..." Mia whimpered softly—her empathy evident in her expression.

"Axle?" Jett called out, his voice echoing the shared unease.

"Everyone lie down again," I gently instructed, hoping to ease their minds. "I'll wake you up when it's time to leave."

But instead of lying down, Harry stepped forward with a determined look. "I'll stand guard and protect everyone," he declared.

I couldn't help but smile at his courage. "Thank you, but you need rest, too. We've had a long journey," I replied, my voice soft with admiration.

"But who'll stand guard?" he asked, his eyes wide with a sense of responsibility far beyond his years.

"I will..." I assured him, my voice steady and comforting.

"Can we lay beside him?" Harry asked, his eyes pleading for reassurance.

"I think he'd enjoy that," I said, watching the little ones gather around him. Once they settled down, the group slowly lowered their heads and drifted back into a peaceful slumber.

Axle looked at me, his eyes speaking volumes of love and gratitude without uttering a single word. Having the babies beside him brought him genuine happiness and comfort in his weariness.

I stood vigil over them, ensuring their safety, as Bobbie-Cat curled against me. As she slept, I remained awake, keeping watch and protecting everyone.

♦♦♦

An eerie stillness settled over the park as the crickets' rhythmic song faded. Startled, I lifted my head and peered into the darkness to see Chief emerging, his presence otherworldly and majestic, shimmering with an ethereal glow. In that instant, I understood—this was his spirit form. My heart clenched as I watched, unable to look away from the surreal vision.

Chief approached Axle, lowered his head, and gently nudged his lifelong friend.

Axle stirred, his tired eyes meeting the gaze of his beloved companion. Recognition dawned on his face, and in that magical moment, a transformation occurred. Axle's earthly shell was left behind, and his spirit rose, vibrant and full of life.

The sight was both beautiful and heartbreaking. Tears welled in my eyes, spilling over as I witnessed their reunion.

Axle and Chief began to play as they once did—tumbling and teasing, their playful banter echoing through the still night air.

Their joy was evident, a testament to the unbreakable bond they shared. Yet, amidst the beauty of their reunion, a deep sorrow nestled in my heart. I sobbed openly as the reality settled that Axle was no longer with us. The bittersweet scene tugged at my heartstrings, leaving me torn between the pain of loss and the comfort of knowing Axle was at peace, surrounded by love in the afterlife.

When they vanished into the darkness, I deeply breathed and whispered goodbye.

A sudden snap of a twig behind me grabbed my attention, and I swung around, fearful of what I might find. Peering into the darkness, I couldn't see anything and stood ready to wake the little ones.

"Molly?"

I gasped, hearing a familiar voice calling my name. My fright diminished as I walked toward the direction of the voice.

In seconds, my beloved Marceau emerged from the woods, coming toward me. This was not his spirit—this was his real self.

Marceau was alive.

"Molly!" he cried, limping excitedly toward me.

I ran to him, happiness evident in my voice. "Oh, Marceau! I thought I lost you…"

The excitement between us woke everyone up. They were overjoyed to see Marceau, but the excitement faded when Axle didn't join in, and the little ones knew something was wrong.

"We've lost him," I explained softly.

"I'm so sorry," Marceau replied, understanding the gravity of the situation.

I returned to the little ones who needed my support, knowing Marceau would understand. Their tears broke my heart. I gathered everyone together, and we mourned his passing.

Marceau stood beside me, providing silent strength.

Although Axle's passing saddened me, Marceau's presence made my heart sing. Turning toward him, I whispered, "How did you get away?"

"I waited for the bear to fall asleep. When he did, I ran away," he explained, a grin lighting up his face. Marceau leaned in and kissed me, and I reciprocated, aware that Axle was smiling from above.

49

BOBBI-CAT

A S WE ENTERED the circus grounds, the morning sky stretched above us in shades of pink and gold. Despite feeling tired from our long journey, everyone radiated excitement about returning home. Elsa spotted her mom by the bonfire and couldn't contain her joy. She lifted her trunk and let out a trumpet blast to announce our arrival. Her mom responded in return, and suddenly, everyone rushed toward us for a heartfelt reunion.

Scanning the crowd, my gaze landed on Cody, nestled in Rosie's arms. The moment our eyes met—he leaped down and raced toward me.

"I was so worried about you," he exclaimed, his voice a tender mix of concern and love. "Why did you leave?"

Looking deep into his eyes, I felt the undeniable pull of his affection. "Oh, Cody," I sighed. "You love performing. Leaving the circus would have shattered your heart."

"You were leaving me?" he asked.

"Yes..." I confessed, the enormity of my decision weighing heavily on me.

"Oh, Bobbie-Cat," he murmured, pulling me into a protective and reassuring embrace. "We belong together. Please, don't ever leave me again."

Before I could respond, the atmosphere shifted dramatically as the ringmaster burst onto the scene, firing a shot into the air to seize everyone's attention.

The crowd froze, gripped by fear and uncertainty.

Spotting Taya holding Mischa by the scruff of her neck, the ringmaster grinned, realizing the profound significance of their return.

"Cage them!" he shouted, pointing at a carnival worker.

But before the worker could move, a mighty grunt broke the stillness, drawing all eyes to Ziya, the male gorilla.

With a commanding presence, Ziya flung open his cage and advanced toward the ringmaster angrily.

Panic-stricken, Philip Andrews raised the gun.

Ziya stood tall, locking eyes with the ringmaster, a silent challenge sparking between them.

When the ringmaster tightened his finger around the trigger, a rush of panic surged through me, and I muttered, "Oh, no..." There was nothing anyone could do—we all stood there, hearts pounding, watching with bated breath.

"Get back in your cage!" the ringmaster shouted, his voice trembling.

Ziya responded to the threat with a powerful display, pounding his chest with a thunderous thump that resonated throughout the circus grounds.

I could see the ringmaster's hand shake—clearly indicating his growing fear. In an instant, he screamed, losing his grip on the gun, which fell to the ground with a heavy thud.

Seizing the opportunity, Ziya charged forward, lifting the ringmaster by the collar. The ringmaster kicked and flailed in a frantic attempt to escape, but it was futile.

As everyone watched in awe, Ziya carried the ringmaster toward his cage, placed him inside, and slammed the door shut.

"The ringmaster's reign is over! Hip, hip, hooray!" shouted the dog-faced boy. Everyone joined in the chorus, their cheers echoing around us.

In the distance, sirens wailed, cutting through the jubilant atmosphere. The chant diminished as police cars sped down the midway, their tires screeching to a halt. Officers jumped from their vehicles, announcing the ringmaster's arrest for illegal firearm possession. With swift efficiency, they handcuffed him, recited his rights, and shoved him into the back of a police car.

As cheers erupted around us once more, I turned to Cody and embraced him. "We don't have to leave now..." I shouted over everyone. He nodded, a warm smile spreading across his face. In that moment, surrounded by laughter and joy, I knew with all my heart that our future was brighter than ever.

◆◆◆

In the center ring, a brilliant spotlight bathed Sofia Bartolini, casting a warm glow that highlighted her poised and confident presence. She stood tall, exuding charisma in a stunning ringmaster's uniform that captivated the audience with its elegance and flair. Her jacket, a deep crimson trimmed with golden braids and buttons, fit her perfectly, accentuating her graceful stance. A matching top hat sat atop her head, adorned with a colorful feather that danced with her every movement.

Sofia beamed at the crowd, her smile as bright as the lights above, as she took a moment to soak in the anticipation thrumming through the tent. Her clear and inviting voice rang out across the audience.

"Ladies and gentlemen, boys and girls!"

The audience applauded, creating a lively atmosphere filled with eager faces and excited whispers.

"The Bellucci Traveling Circus is proud to present our newest and most delightful act..." Sofia announced, her words punctuated by the rising tempo of a drum roll echoing through the space, building suspense. She paused, letting the anticipation reach a fever pitch before revealing, "MARCEAU AND THE ACROBATIC PUPPIES!"

Marceau strode into the spotlight, offering a theatrical bow that earned him an appreciative round of applause. He gestured dramatically toward a charming cardboard doghouse painted whimsically with bright colors and intricate patterns.

Another drum roll began, each beat syncing with the spectators' pounding hearts. The doghouse door swung open at its climactic finish and out trotted six of the most adorable puppies imaginable. Each puppy, a bundle of fur and boundless energy, bounded into the ring, tails wagging furiously.

The audience gasped collectively—their hearts captured by the sight of these charming little creatures.

The puppies, each with their unique coat of spots and patterns, performed playful antics and synchronized tricks that showcased their agility and training. They leaped through hoops and scampered over small obstacles with such endearing charm that the audience couldn't help but respond with infectious laughter and applause.

As the act concluded, my heart brimmed with excitement, and I dashed out of the tent, racing down the bustling midway toward the nursery.

The "Morton's Nursery" sign welcomed me as I stepped inside, where laughter and playful sounds filled the air. Instantly, I was drawn to an enchanting sight—Elsa swaying Morton at the tip of her trunk. Like a whimsical rollercoaster, she lifted him up and down, embodying the pure joy of the moment.

Morton's face radiated happiness, his eyes alight with delight and love, and his dramatic flair ignited smiles and giggles among the babies.

Elsa's heart swelled with affection as she carefully lowered Morton to the ground, her eyes twinkling with the warmth of love. Just then, a baby male giraffe graced the scene, his elegant form towering majestically beside Mia.

Mia gazed affectionately at the giraffe, her voice soft and tender. "I love you, little brother," she said, her words rich with pride, reflecting their deep familial bond.

Suddenly, a gentle cry echoed in the background, stirring concern. I turned to find Mischa nestled in a cozy straw bed, trembling with remnants of a nightmare. Just as I contemplated offering comfort, a breathtaking sight unfolded. The majestic spirit form of Axle materialized. He exuded soothing energy, gliding gracefully to Mischa's side.

Mischa's distress faded, and a serene smile replaced it, shining like a beacon of comfort and peace—a testament to the mystical presence of her spectral guardian.

As I transitioned into my role as Sofia's dedicated assistant, I ensured everything ran smoothly and everyone was content. Sofia entrusted me with this position, elevating me from a "rat catcher" to a vital part of the circus family.

Satisfied that all was well in Morton's Nursery, I bid the babies farewell and rushed back to the big top, eager not to miss Molly's grand performance. As I slipped back into the tent, the air was filled with anticipation.

Molly commanded the ring, her form a blur of motion and grace. The audience was enraptured, eyes wide and breaths held, as she executed a series of breathtaking front flips and backflips, her movements fluid and precise. With each leap, she defied gravity, her flexibility, and agility drawing gasps of awe from the spectators.

The crowd erupted into thunderous applause. Their admiration for Molly was evident in the resounding claps and cheers that filled the tent.

Molly's radiant smile beamed back at them, reflecting her triumphant spirit.

As the applause subsided, Molly stepped onto a platform, her expression focused on determination. The platform rose slowly, elevating her into the heart of the big top.

The air grew thick with suspense, and the audience held their breath, fully aware that she was about to perform a heart-stopping, life-defying act.

With my heart in my throat, I watched Molly with bated breath, awe and concern swirling within me as the tent fell into a hushed silence. Every eye was locked on her, the anticipation almost tangible as she prepared to perform her next daring feat.

The platform halted, and with it, a spotlight singled out Molly, casting her in a glow of pure anticipation. She rose gracefully onto her hind legs, lifting her right paw in a playful salute to the captivated audience below, her eyes sparkling with an infectious joy.

As the drum roll crescendoed and ceased, the tent was enveloped in a breathless silence.

Molly sprang into the air, her form a picture of elegance.

The audience collectively held its breath, entranced by her majestic dive toward the ground.

Molly began a series of flawless flips in mid-air, each rotation a testament to her skill and bravery before she plunged seamlessly into a pool of water.

The surface erupted in a shimmer of droplets as Molly emerged triumphantly, standing once more on her hind legs.

In a grand, climactic finale, she lifted her right paw, her face glowing with happiness and pride, as the audience burst into an uproar of applause and cheers.

Marceau and the puppies rushed into the ring, embracing Molly joyfully.

Overcome with emotion, Molly's eyes glistened with tears of joy, her heart swelling with the crowd's love and admiration.

50

FRANK

AS GEORGE AND I journeyed with the circus through the countryside, I was filled with joy watching Sofia Bartolini excel as the ringmaster. Her leadership ensured the animals were respected and the performers received fair pay.

After an extensive tour, the announcement of our return to New Orleans sparked a wave of excitement, and we eagerly anticipated revisiting the Crescent City.

Upon arrival, Billy-Joe joined our ranks, and I was surprised by his remarkable transformation. His improved hygiene, clean uniform, new teeth, and respectful demeanor contrasted with his past. By voluntarily contacting the police and admitting to their wrongdoing, he reduced his sentence.

Sofia, recognizing his genuine remorse and understanding that Sam was the true mastermind behind the kidnapping and Chief's tragic death, agreed to take Billy-Joe back. However, she withheld her compassion for Sam, now serving a lengthy, well-deserved prison sentence.

With the circus back in town, I enlisted George to help spread the word about our return and Sofia's new leadership role.

Surprisingly, the usually grumpy George was brimming with joyful enthusiasm, eager to share the exciting news.

"Yes! Let's spread the word," he exclaimed, his voice rising excitedly.

Just as I was ready to take flight, George mentioned a quick stop, leaving me puzzled.

"If we're going to party, we need music!" he declared.

I grinned, nodding in agreement.

George took off, and I followed.

He spotted a boom box, swooped down, and grabbed it.

The music playing didn't quite fit the celebratory mood. "May I?" I asked, flying alongside him.

"Please..." he replied, understanding my intention.

As we soared, I turned the dial until an upbeat disco tune blared, transforming the somber atmosphere.

Grinning, George started swaying to the rhythm of Chic's classic song "Everybody Dance."

I cranked up the volume.

Below, everyone looked up from the circus grounds, drawn to the music.

"It's time for a celebration!" I called out with a flourish, beckoning everyone to join in the merriment.

The circus grounds came alive as everyone swayed and danced to the lively music.

I enthusiastically joined in, moving to the rhythm with exaggerated flair. But just as I reached the peak of my dance performance, an unexpected sound escaped from my derriere—a loud and unmistakable fluffer-doodle. I froze briefly, eyes wide with surprise, then glanced around sheepishly.

Everyone paused below, and then laughter erupted, rippling through the gathering like a jubilant wave.

"Oops..." I murmured, blushing furiously.

Sophia, quick to see the humor, doubled over with laughter.

Ziya clapped his massive hands in delight, amused by the unexpected musical addition.

Even the babies, sensing the light-hearted mood, giggled uncontrollably.

My best friend, George, started giggling softly, then erupted into loud laughter, nearly dropping the boom box.

"Oh, Frank... Life would be so boring without you!" he chortled.

As the laughter ended, the dance party began.

The large male poodle and the Scottish terrier started doing the "bump" dance in perfect harmony.

I smiled at little Mischa, watching her energetically pump her paws. Her enthusiasm lit up Taya's face as she clapped along.

As Maddie and little Capo twirled together, Capo's joyful squeals echoed around them, filling his mother's heart with joy. Behind them, Chief's spirit sat majestically, a proud smile beaming as he watched over them.

More performers joined the gathering.

Rosie and the "World's Tallest Man" danced beside each other, their eyes reflecting their blossoming relationship. Rosie's cheeks were a rosy hue, blushing with happiness.

Elsa, Harry, Jett, and Mia danced together, their smiles showcasing the joy of friendship as their parents grooved alongside them.

Morton danced with flair—his moves reminiscent of John Travolta's iconic style. His hips swayed with precision, and his steps were sharp and rhythmic, exuding confidence. As he spun around, his arms pumped energetically above him, capturing the vibrant spirit of the moment.

Sophia and the "Strongman" boogied with smiles and laughter.

Molly and the puppies danced together while Marceau looked on proudly.

Bobbie-Cat beamed joyfully, dancing alongside Cody, his love for her evident.

Everyone participated in the celebration except for Felicia. Because of her large belly, she reclined on the sidelines, unable to join the festivities. As she fanned herself, her face showed a mix of irritability and frustration with the consequences of her actions.

Our flock joined us as we flew toward Audubon Park to spread the news. Flying over the zoo, Luca glanced up and began dancing. His family surrounded him, clapping their hands in celebration.

The Rhesus Macaque monkeys joined in—their playful energy contagious as they swayed with their arms waving rhythmically. They leaped from one foot to another, bouncing and twirling in circles.

Once Bird Island came into view, we landed and started the festivities there, too. All the birds on the island, along with Sadie and the alligators, danced under the soft glimmer of lightning bugs.

A profound sense of happiness and peace washed over me as I looked around at the joy and unity enveloping us. We danced in unison to the rhythm of life, creating a cherished moment—an ending that heralded the promise of a new beginning.

The End

ACKNOWLEDGMENT

"Circus Animals" began as a screenplay I wrote many years ago, a project close to my heart that evolved over time. The warm reception and accolades it received inspired me to transform it into a novel, allowing me to share this cherished story with an even wider audience.

To my esteemed colleagues, your expertise and guidance were instrumental in shaping this work. Your dedication and meticulous attention to detail have not gone unnoticed, and I am profoundly grateful for your contributions.

I extend a special tribute to all the pets I've loved over the years, whose names grace the pages of this novel. This is my way of honoring their lasting impact on my life and acknowledging the joy they've brought me.

Lastly, thank you to my friends and family. Your support has made this accomplishment possible, and I am eternally grateful.

Frank Gaimari

ABOUT THE AUTHOR

Frank Gaimari

Hailing from the Pacific Northwest, Frank Gaimari is an esteemed writer and painter who has captivated a global audience with his skill in crafting intricate and compelling narratives, earning him numerous accolades. Frank's artistic prowess enhances his writing, lending a unique visual dimension. Beyond his creative pursuits, he is a devoted family man, cherishing his roles as a husband and stepfather to his two extraordinary sons. His family is completed by two beloved golden retrievers who hold a special place in his heart.

www.FrankGaimari.com.
FrankGaimariAuthor@gmail.com

www.ingramcontent.com/pod-product-compliance
Lightning Source LLC
Chambersburg PA
CBHW070502300726
48975CB00007B/2284